LOVE, LIES AND LAVENDER

A Blueberry Point Romance Book 1

D.E. MALONE

Love, Lies and Lavender
Copyright © 2020 D.E. Malone. All rights reserved.
ISBN (paperback) 978-1-951516-03-1
(ebook) 978-1-951516-04-8
Cover design by Blue Water Books
First Edition

For the latest book happenings, special subscriber giveaways, and advance notice on sales and new releases, please subscribe to my newsletter.

Chapter One

The ground seemed to sway underneath Hilary Larkin's feet as she stepped through the gate in Duluth International Airport. She made her way to the main corridor, setting her sights on the *Welcome to Minnesota!* kiosk ahead. The flight had been awful. Flying was the worst on a *good* day.

Tugging her suitcase beside her, Hilary took a deep breath and immediately regretted it. The smell of diesel and fried foods from Big Jim's BBQ across the way wasn't the best combination for her already nauseous stomach. While she tried to get her bearings, the other passengers from her flight dispersed in all directions like a disturbed anthill.

Her phone dinged. She took it out of her pocket. The screen lit up with a message from her sister-in-law Jorie.

Missed the flight. I'll send an update later. Sorry.

Hilary shook her head. Running late was such a Jorie thing, but it wasn't her fault this time. Jorie's father— Hilary's father-in-law—came down with pneumonia last week and was hospitalized two days ago, tossing all plans in the air. Cal Larkin's health took precedence over some conference. Hilary would make the best of it and cross her fingers Jorie could catch another flight as soon as possible.

She checked the overhead sign once again and headed down the long corridor. The flight had been on time despite the rough start. She had fifteen minutes to find her suitcase before the pick-up time listed on her itinerary. As she walked, her lightheadedness faded. She concentrated on the click of her boots on the tile floor and grumbled to herself about her dislike for airports. Ahead, the corridor intersected with the baggage claim area. She stopped to scan yet another overhead sign, this time noting the carousel numbers, until she found the one connected with her flight.

She set her shoulder bag at her feet and stuck her hands in her coat pockets to wait. A few dozen people were already there.

"Are you here for the farm conference?"

She'd been so busy stewing about being here alone, especially since Jorie signed her up for this, that she didn't sense anyone nearby.

Hilary turned. The young woman who'd sat across the aisle from her on the flight from Grand Forks stood there. Her upbeat voice and friendly face were contagious. Hilary smiled back.

"Yes. First time in Minnesota too." How did the woman know she was here for the conference? Then it dawned on her. Larkin Farms was embroidered across the back of her jacket.

"Where are you from?" the woman asked.

Hilary cleared her throat. "A town not too far from Boise called Redville." Her voice cracked. She hadn't done much talking since boarding the flight at six that morning.

"I grew up in the northern part of Minnesota but live in North Dakota now," the woman said.

Hilary nodded. She wasn't very good at the chitchat.

They stood in silence for a few minutes, watching the cavernous mouth with the black strips of rubber part as suitcases rolled toward them on the belt. Hilary watched for the blue length of satin ribbon she'd tied to her suitcase handle.

"Here's mine." The woman stopped the bag on the belt before heaving it over the edge and onto the floor. "I'll wait for you."

Relief eased the anxious knot in her stomach. Hilary wouldn't have to wander through this strange airport alone, looking for the contact person.

"I'm Meg, by the way. Meg Willson."

"Hilary Larkin. Nice to meet you." Now that they faced one another, Hilary recognized the pin Meg wore on the lapel of her blazer right away. The white-and-gold ear of corn on a red background. The Gold Standard Seed decal. Her husband had sold their products. Hilary swallowed hard and looked away.

Meg went on. "My family raises sheep and a small herd of alpacas. My mother is a fiber artist. And Mom found out there's a fiber artist at the conference too, so she's over the moon about that." Meg looked around. "She's here somewhere. Must still be in the restroom." She shrugged and leaned on the handle of her suitcase. "Anyway, we hosted a holiday open house in our refurbished barn. *Huge* turnout last November at the start of the Christmas season. So that got us thinking about expanding. You know, giving classes on spinning, weaving, hosting artist groups. Stuff like that."

Hilary exhaled through her nose. While thankful for Meg's company, she could do with a little less conversation. Her bag finally appeared on the belt, the blue ribbon a beacon of relief. She stepped forward to claim it, lugging its weight onto the floor. It landed with a thud.

Meg looked down at the suitcase. She giggled. "I have a tendency to overpack too. It's a security thing. You know, bringing those familiar comforts to offset the stress of being somewhere new."

The woman was trying to be helpful, but Hilary didn't need the reminder that home was fifteen-hundred miles away. Her hand clutching the suitcase handle was moist. Jorie owed her big.

Meg waved to someone across the room. "There's my mom. You'll have to meet her."

Meg's mother, Yandi, lumbered over a few seconds later, dragging a black orthopedic boot. She shook Hilary's hand with a crushingly enthusiastic grip. The woman was taller than her willowy daughter. Hilary flexed her hand at her side, feeling the bones settle back into their rightful places.

"I think we need to make our way to the front entrance. We're looking for someone with a 'Small Farms Conference/BPL' sign," said Meg, looking at the paper she'd pulled from her coat pocket.

"What's BPL?" asked Yandi.

"Blueberry Point Lodge. The place that's hosting the conference," Hilary offered. The only bright spot of this conference she looked forward to so far was staying in the historic lodge. The place boasted gourmet meals, premium mattresses, and a short walk off the back patio to Lake Superior. If she could pretend it was a vacation instead of work, she'd be set.

"Oh, that's right. The insane hour I got up this morning finally caught up to me," Yandi said, palming her forehead. She shooed them to get going. "Don't let me hold you back. This bum foot isn't going to slow me down too much."

Hilary hung back while the two women talked about how clean the airport seemed and marveled at the golden croton plants in gigantic earthen pots. Hilary felt like a third wheel. The Invisible Woman. The *Irritated*, Invisible Woman, that was.

Stop feeling sorry for yourself. You could have turned Jorie down. It's your own fault.

Following the signs, the three of them walked from baggage claim toward the front entrance. The wall of glass before them revealed a wide blue sky, a stark contrast to the dreary gray day Hilary left behind in Idaho.

"Oh, I think I see our contact person," said Yandi.

Meg waved. "Yep, that's him."

Hilary's phone dinged again.

Earliest I can catch the next flight is Wednesday. Worst week already and it's only Sunday. Ugh.

Her heart sank. That was half the conference. If she felt out of her element at signing up for a small farms conference before, this spelled doom for her morale. Her sister-in-law was Miss Owyhee County Ag Queen in high school. Born into the farm life, Jorie lived and breathed it. Hilary, on the other hand, was voted Most Likely to Live in a High Rise. This was Jorie's thing, not hers.

Hilary craned her neck to see over the two tall women in front of her to no avail and looked again at her phone to read the rest of Jorie's message. But Meg stopped and her suitcase almost tripped Hilary.

"I'm kind of dangerous with this thing. Sorry," Meg said, swinging the suitcase to her side. She stepped aside for Hilary.

As Hilary struggled to correct the bag handle that caught on the shoulder flap of her jacket, she caught a glimpse of the man waiting for them with the BPL sign held against his chest.

She slowed.

He looked so familiar. The mop of russet hair, tousled like he'd tumbled out of bed moments ago, threw her off. Yes, of course. The hair. Its color reminded her of Will's, though it was a few shades lighter. She stared a little too hard for a little too long and the man did a double take, probably trying to gauge her.

As much as she wanted to look away, she couldn't bring herself to do it. His soulful eyes studied her and widened when she gave him a quick smile. The shadow of a not-quite beard trailed along his jaw, thicker in spots than others. Even from the distance, she noted his jeans were worn at the knees, yet his plaid shirt still held the yellow size sticker over his left pocket. She smiled again despite her sour mood.

Another message from Jorie appeared.

Not sure it's worth me coming if I'm missing half the conference.

Hilary sighed. What else could go wrong today? First,

her no-show sister-in-law abandons her at a conference Hilary didn't want to come to in the first place, and now Will's doppelgänger was here to meet her in the terminal?

This was a fantastic start to her week away from home.

Chapter Two

❧❦❧

Dane Porter wheeled into the nearest empty spot in the short-term parking lot and unbuckled his belt. He jumped out, clicked the lock near the door handle, then noticed the ignition sensor yelling at him to pull the keys out. *That* would have been bad.

Of course he was late. The Stetmans trusted him to pick up a few of the last-minute arrivals for the Small Farms and Sustainability Conference, even loaned him their car, and he was late.

Judging by the parking lot, the airport was busy. He hurried through the rows, almost breaking into a run before he realized he forgot the sign. The conference people would never find him with it still in the backseat.

Get it together, Dane.

He'd been rehearsing his keynote speech for

tomorrow morning on the drive from Hendricks. Encouraging words, anecdotes of farm life, and the pitfalls of being a small business owner filled his head. The speech was all over the place. It didn't feel cohesive. He'd have to work on it tonight when he was back in his room at Blueberry Point Lodge.

Inside the airport, a light-filled space with soaring glass walls and ceilings, he stopped. Somewhere four people probably wondered if they were stranded here indefinitely. He should have been here a half hour ago. He looked around for a place to stand out of the way of the crowd streaming past him and found a spot near an empty kiosk. Leaning against the kiosk, Dane caught sight of himself in a mirrored pillar nearby. His hair looked like the spiky wet coat of Poe after the dog took a swim in the pond and shook off excess water. Dane smoothed it with a hurried hand and looked around.

They spotted him first. Two very tall women waved to him in unison. One was a smilier, slimmer version of the other woman, obviously a mother-daughter team. They carried on an animated conversation together as they approached Dane, gesturing wildly with their free hands, pulling wheeled suitcases with the others.

The older woman bent forward to peer at his cardboard sign, sounding out the name in exaggerated syllables. "S-mall F-arms Con-fer-ence. Nice to meet you, Small Farms Conference," she said. Her daughter watched her with a mixture of amusement and embarrassment.

"I'm sorry I'm late," Dane said. "There's no excuse. Darcy and Sean Stetman are helping acclimate the other guests back in Hendricks. They asked me to make a run here."

The younger woman waved him off and set the bag she held on top of her suitcase. "Not a biggie. I'm Meg. This is my mother, Yandi."

He still held the sign across his chest like a goon and dropped it to his side. "Do you need help with your bags?"

Yandi stood stooped over the handle of her suitcase, resting. It was then that Dane noticed the woman behind them.

The first thought that flashed through his mind was that she looked really irritated. The skin between two finely arched brows was pinched. She almost looked like she sported a pretty intense migraine with the way she kept pressing on her temple with two fingers. But peeved expressions aside, she was gorgeous. Her eyes were the color of the pond back home when it froze over and the sky above glinted off its cold surface. Like blue-gray ice. They almost overwhelmed her face and certainly her nose, which was small and pinched. She scanned her surroundings—the check-in desk, the replica biplane suspended from the ceiling, the family of four with a screaming toddler hurrying past them on their way to the parking lot. And then her gaze rested on him.

His heart nearly stopped. If it weren't for the commotion of the busy airport around him, he might have fallen into the deep well of those eyes. They simultaneously made him grow cold with gooseflesh and heated his face until he felt his hair had surely caught fire. Something about her reminded him of the lavender fields back home too.

She blinked as if she'd just noticed him.

"Hi there." His voice came out hoarse, uneven. Dane cleared his throat and tried again. "I'm Dane." He doubted she'd heard him the first time.

"Hilary Larkin." She smiled crookedly, but it disappeared as fast as it materialized when her bag slipped and she jerked to catch it. She groaned impatiently, hitching it onto her shoulder again.

"Can I carry that for you?"

"No, thanks," she said curtly, looking away.

Dane mentally shook himself. If she was upset about waiting, he didn't blame her. Being late wasn't a good first impression.

"We should be getting back," he said to the group. "There's a full day planned with only a half day left."

"Fine by me," Yandi said. "I've been itching for this conference all winter."

"My sister-in-law didn't make it after all."

He looked back at Hilary. Her voice was so soft he was

surprised he caught the words. It registered then that there *were* only three of them. He'd been so taken aback by her that he hadn't noticed that rather important detail. If he got through this week without Darcy chewing him out for not being on top of his game, it'd be miraculous.

"What happened?" he asked as the four of them exited the terminal. She walked behind him so he slowed to wait for her to catch up.

"Something came up back home." She shrugged. The breeze ruffled her chestnut hair, sending a strand across her lips. She brushed it away, but it floated across her face again.

Dane waited for her to elaborate, but she didn't add anything. *So she's not into oversharing. Fine. Neither was he.* Besides, he didn't trust his voice not to crack again. It was a two-hour trip back to Hendricks. There was plenty of time to regain his composure. He cringed inwardly at the thought. Why was his composure an issue anyway?

He loaded suitcases into the back of the SUV, and they were on the road in no time. Dane found a station playing easy rock and turned the volume down. Meg and Yandi were in the backseat, talking over one another in their excitement. Next to him, Hilary sat quietly.

The suburban landscape soon gave way to a wide-open stretch of highway with Lake Superior on their right, glistening in the late-morning sun. He'd like living near the Big Lake if his life had taken another direction. He felt a sense of wildness looking at it now, like he was without constraints. Free. But his life back on the farm in Clove was pretty idyllic. He was his own boss now that his parents were almost fully retired, and the business had grown a thousandfold from when Mom started growing lavender in the garden to sell at the farmer's market twenty years ago.

Dane glanced in the rearview mirror. Meg and Yandi had their heads together, looking down.

"So what brings everyone to the conference anyway?"

Yandi jumped on his question right away, giving the full business plan for their sheep and alpaca farm in animated detail. They were like a comedy team duo. Dane found himself laughing while casting glances at Hilary in the passenger seat. She continued to look out the window, but from her profile he could see a small grin.

"What about you?" he asked Hilary when there was a break in the conversation. She'd been listening but hadn't spoken since they got in the car at the airport.

Hilary looked at him, surprised. "I—ah, we grow wheat. Near Redville. That's in Idaho."

We. He'd noticed the wedding ring.

"So you're looking to capitalize on that or head in another direction?"

Her hands, already in her lap, clasped together. She rubbed her thumb with the other.

"My sister-in-law dreams of operating a B & B. She and her husband bought some adjacent land with an old house and an orchard too." Hilary shrugged. "I guess we're planning on opening the B & B." She shrugged again.

"Oh, an apple orchard..." said Yandi. "What we couldn't do with one of those."

Meg snorted. "When was the last time you baked, Momma?"

"Last weekend. Though you'd never know it the way Henry and the boys tear through my treats. Why are you giving me a hard time? If I want to dream about apple orchards, leave me be."

That started another round of good-natured sniping in the backseat. Dane listened, smiling. It reminded him of when he and his two brothers were younger, fighting over the last slice of pie or brownie in the pan. Now Ben and Rafe were living in the city, Ben in Seattle, and Rafe in Portland, a long way from the farm in terms of miles and lifestyle. Dane couldn't imagine. He was a homebody.

He glanced over at Hilary. "And your sister-in-law isn't here. That's kind of a problem."

Another shrug.

"So, you two will partner up on this new venture?"

A small nod. "That's the idea."

"How did you end up on the North Dakota flight if you came from Boise? Direct flights weren't available?"

"My sister-in-law booked connecting flights to save money." Hilary shook her head and turned toward the window again, watching the landscape pass by. "Funny, now she'll pay more in the long run," she mumbled. "If she decides to come."

Maybe he should stop asking questions. He was beginning to feel intrusive; she didn't want to share anything beyond answering his questions in as few words as possible. Besides, Yandi and Meg had no trouble carrying on the conversation for all of them.

They pulled into the gravel drive at Blueberry Point Lodge at a quarter till twelve. Darcy had ordered sack lunches for the tour group, which she loaded into the bus in gray totes when Dane pulled in nearby. He unlocked the hatch again and deposited bags on the ground. Hilary's were the last ones in the SUV.

"I can get mine," she said as she heaved her suitcase from the back. Her shoulder bag bumped him as she maneuvered the heavier luggage.

Dane stepped back. "No problem."

She didn't acknowledge him and was already walking toward Darcy and the larger group, suitcase trailing behind her.

Dane shut the lift gate. He watched her retreating back. He couldn't help but wonder if he hadn't said something to turn her off. He huffed. No, he had to stop thinking like that. Always shouldering the blame wasn't healthy. Sometimes it was on the other person.

Chapter Three

H ilary gazed up at Blueberry Point Lodge as
she trudged toward the entrance with Meg
and her mother. It was one of the grandest
buildings she'd ever seen, all chimneys and windows and
one of those carport things she imagined had sheltered
its share of guests arriving for fancy events long ago. And
the view of the lake was stunning. The back of the house
faced the water and while she couldn't see it yet, she
knew whoever built this house had taken full advantage
of that view.

Pea gravel crunched under her feet as she pulled the
suitcase along behind her. It was a lonely sound, her
solitary footsteps. Jorie should have been there. This was
never something she intended to do by herself, attend a
farming conference. Maybe her hosts wouldn't miss her if
she stayed in her room until Jorie arrived.

Don't be ridiculous. You can do this.

Getting off the farm actually felt good. She hadn't left it much since the accident. Jorie and her husband had been dropping hints and invitations for months. "Come with us to Spokane for the weekend. We're taking the trailer," Jorie offered early last spring. Hilary immediately dismissed the idea, telling her it was way too soon. Then over Thanksgiving weekend, Jorie tried again. "How about we check out that new B & B near Kennewick? We'll write it off as a business expense." That didn't happen either. Each time they offered to take her somewhere, Hilary was armed with an excuse. Then Jorie showed her the webpage for Blueberry Point Lodge and the conference for small farmers scheduled for this summer. Hilary realized something changed inside her because her knee-jerk response to say "no" didn't happen. But that was before Jorie missed the flight. Now Hilary was stranded hundreds of miles away in a strange place, and the only place she wanted to be was home.

"Welcome, ladies!"

Hilary startled.

The black-haired woman she'd seen loading a tub into the tour bus in the parking lot caught up to them.

"I'm Darcy Stetman, your hostess for the week. I'll show you to your rooms so you can drop off your things, then we'll need to make a quick transition for the Hendricks tour."

"Actually, I'm not feeling all that well," Hilary blurted.

"Headache. From traveling." If she could beg off for the afternoon, she'd check in with Jorie. Maybe grab a nap too.

Darcy, Meg, and Yandi cried out some variation of "Oh no!"

"You can't," said Meg. "This is the equivalent of happy hour."

"I think I need to. I'd hate to be coming down with something and have to miss more of the week." Hilary kept her head down. If she looked at them, they might talk her into coming along.

Darcy touched her arm. "We'd hate for you to miss it. Are you sure?"

Yandi shook her bag, rattling its contents. "I have something for headaches."

"I'm sure. I hope to be well for the dinner tonight. If I can lay down for an hour, I'll be as good as new."

"That's too bad," Darcy said. "But I understand. There's nothing worse than being away from home when you're not feeling well."

Thank goodness. She hated starting the week off on the wrong foot, but she really needed to get her head straightened out. A couple hours and a check-in with Jorie after she unpacked might do the trick.

HILARY STOOD AT ONE OF THE TALL WINDOWS IN her bedroom, watching the tour group assemble in the driveway below. It was a larger group than she expected. Yandi and Meg were in the middle, no doubt having one of their loud, animated conversations. And that Dane guy was near them too. She felt a twinge of guilt for being so abrupt with him. He seemed to be trying hard to engage her in conversation earlier, but all she wanted was to ride in peace during the two-hour trip to Hendricks. The feeling she'd had when she saw him was uncanny. Now that she could study him without reservation, he looked nothing like Will. Yet there was something about him.

Another tour bus with a fiberglass fish arrived to carry the passenger overload from the first bus. Hilary smiled in spite of her mood. The paint job on the buses was a patchwork of neon lettering in lime green—STURGEON WIDOWS TOURS!—and kitschy graphics. For a second she regretted her choice to stay behind. With branding like that, the tour itself was probably a riot.

She let the curtain drop back in place and fell onto the plush bed, the phone ringing in her ear. Of course Jorie took her time answering, even though she carried her phone on her every waking moment. Jorie always had a million things going on at once.

When she finally answered, her sister-in-law was breathless.

"Hil, thank goodness. I've been trying to call," Jorie said.

Funny, her phone hadn't registered any calls. She'd

check again when they hung up. Maybe service in Hendricks was iffy.

"What's up?"

In the background, Hattie's high-pitched squeals carried over the phone line as if she wasn't hundreds of miles away. Hattie was probably in her high chair, throwing parts of her lunch to Rowdy. Hilary pictured the dog standing vigilant like he always did, keeping the floor clean like a four-legged vacuum.

"Nothing here. Just the usual chaos," Jorie said. "But now that you're settled, how's it going?"

Hilary wouldn't exactly call herself settled, but it was nice to hear Jorie's concern.

"It's beautiful here. The people I've met have been really nice." She tried to keep her voice upbeat.

"What's on your agenda today? I've forgotten what they had lined up for us."

"There's a tour now and dinner later on."

"You're on a tour now?" Jorie asked. "It's so quiet."

"Not me. I stayed behind."

"Why aren't you going?"

"I needed some down time."

"The plane ride and drive wasn't enough?"

"Jorie." Hilary couldn't suppress the warning tone. Sometimes Jorie took things too far.

Hilary heard Jorie sigh. The corners of her mouth were probably drooping too once she pressed her lips together. The visual was solidly in Hilary's mind; she'd seen it a thousand times.

The clatter of dishes sounded in the background. Then Jorie coughed.

"Okay, sorry. I was hoping you'd totally embrace this." Jorie's voice was softer now. Hattie's squealing was muted like Jorie moved into another room.

Hilary rolled over onto her stomach. She picked at one of the chenille dots on the bedspread. "I know. I-I'm feeling a little off right now. Sis, I counted on you being here too."

"You know I've looked forward to this for months," Jorie said.

"Yeah, I know. How's your dad?"

"Better. Stabilized. They might release him tomorrow. We'll see."

It was selfish feeling this way. Cal Larkin was a force, always had been, especially for her during the last two years. But here she was thinking of herself when he was laid up in the hospital. Despite the work she, Jorie, and Jorie's husband—Tom—put in at Larkin Farms, it was still Cal's place. He'd rebuilt the farm many times over on the foundation his father laid before he passed away when Cal was barely out of high school.

Silence stretched over the next several seconds while Hilary gazed through the parted curtains across the room. Sunlight grazed the polished surface of the Queen Anne table in front of the window. It was a beautiful early summer day even though she bet the temperatures still hovered in the fifties. A Northwoods summer.

"So maybe you'll come after all? If he's better?"

Hilary wondered if she'd lost the connection since Jorie didn't say anything. But then she heard Hattie in the background.

"I think I'd better stay here."

Hilary pressed her lips together. Jorie wasn't coming. What else was there to say?

"Hilary?"

She closed her eyes. "What?"

"I know you're disappointed."

"Yeah."

"Just think of Will," Jorie said after a moment. Her voice was barely above a whisper now. "He dreamed about expanding the farm for so long."

Hilary's breath came out in a near gasp. She sat upright. Jorie had a way of bringing up Will in her most vulnerable times.

"I know that. I was married to him, remember?" Anger surged in her.

"Of course. It's just—"

"Not now please."

"Hilary, honey, I'm sorry. You need to push forward, as hard as it is. I know he's cheering for you."

"I have to go."

"Wait, Hilary."

Hilary closed her eyes, focusing on keeping the ire from her voice. "What?"

"I really am sorry I can't be there. It doesn't make sense to buy another ticket. I've already lost the money on this one. And Dad's going to need rest for a week at least. There's work to be done here."

"I know." But that wasn't the reason she didn't feel like talking anymore. First, Cal's health kept her from coming. Now, the ticket price was her reason for missing the conference. If Jorie stuck with *one* excuse for missing the conference, it might have been more credible.

Jorie sighed. "I wish there was another solution."

More beats of silence passed. Jorie needed to stay on the farm, not come to a conference across the country. Maybe she didn't need Jorie here after all, especially since she'd just used Hilary's late husband to make a point.

"Do what you think is best."

Hilary hung up while Jorie started to say something else. She couldn't listen anymore. The breaths came out in little gasps while she sat on the edge of the bed, her phone ringing again as Jorie called back. Hilary silenced the phone. She focused on the nubby carpet beneath her feet, the scent of lavender coming from somewhere in the room, and the sound of rushing water when she turned on the faucet in the adjoining bathroom. The water on her face was shockingly cold, yet it soothed her. She stood over the sink for a few minutes, letting the water cascade through her hands. When she looked into the ornate oval mirror above the sink, Hilary scowled at her reflection. An inky trail of mascara rode down her cheek.

Yes, Will would have wanted her to embrace this week. She didn't need Jorie telling her that. But as blunt as Jorie could be sometimes, Hilary knew she meant well.

This was something she'd have to get through, like the other challenges she'd faced since two Aprils ago. But she hadn't counted on doing it alone this time.

Chapter Four

Dane leaned back in his chair, hooking his hands behind his head. He closed his eyes and let gravity work the kinks out of his shoulders. Too much sitting today. He wasn't used to it.

The conference welcome party was in full swing. The ring of clinking glasses from the bar carried across the inside of the enormous tent erected on the lawn of Blueberry Point Lodge. Tables were set for dozens of conference attendees as well as the presenters who'd come for the week. Outside, the sky still held a rosy glow, but it was dark enough now for the string lights hanging from the tent poles to illuminate faces and the amazing dinner spread on two long tables.

"What did you think of the tour?"

It was Darcy. She'd snuck up behind him to plant her hands on his shoulders, giving him a much-too-short massage, before plunking herself into the empty seat beside him. Dane hadn't had the chance to talk with her since he flew in late last night.

"Fun, interesting. Sean's a decent narrator. Between the backwoods humor and his knowledge of Great Lakes shipwrecks, you'll be booking tours and rooms for as long as you can stand it." He unclasped his hands and set them in his lap. "You've really got a nice gig going on here."

"Yeah, I got pretty lucky." She glanced around the tent, taking it all in. "Everything really came together after I took the job as a tour host three years ago."

He found Sean Stetman, Darcy's husband, near the front of the buffet line serving guests as they lined up for the food. "So Sean's family welcomed you into the fold okay?"

Darcy laughed, a throaty sound he remembered from the first day he met her at the Great Lakes Naval Station for boot camp. Her laugh turned heads with its gusto, that was for sure.

"Oh my gosh, yes," Darcy said, nodding. "Honestly, they've been like family to me since day one. Did you know Sean's great-grandfather built this place? It was out of the family for a few decades. Then Sean helped his parents snatch it up when it went on the market again."

They shared a love of old buildings. This one was a masterpiece. "They're lucky to get it back."

"I'm just relieved we were able to save it from ruin," Darcy said. "It was in terrible shape."

Dane leaned forward to see out from under the tent awning to the house's roof. Slate tiles—nice. Those chimneys were pretty impressive too. Man, he bet the place cost a fortune in upkeep. He guessed the North Shore tourism industry was thriving. Not that Darcy wasn't self-sufficient, but he was happy to know she lived comfortably, working at something she loved.

After meeting Darcy during basic training, they'd remained good friends even after their time was up and they returned to civilian life. He'd been asked many times by friends why they'd never dated. Each time he'd remind them he had a girlfriend. And strange as it was, he wasn't attracted to Darcy *that* way. Darcy felt more like a sister.

She leaned over to lay her hand on his arm. "Enough about me. It's been forever since we talked about anything other than this conference. Thanks for agreeing to present, by the way. I don't think I can thank you enough."

"I wouldn't have missed it." After a long winter, he'd been ready to mingle with some like-minded people anyway.

"And thank you for bringing these," she said, cupping her hand around the lavender-filled Mason jar arrangement. "They smell heavenly."

He'd shipped the fresh-cut lavender blooms last week.

She'd paired them with some tiny white flowers he didn't recognize.

Dane shrugged, grinning at her. "I get them at cost."

"So, the lavender business is booming?"

"It is. Can't complain."

"Are your brothers still involved?"

Dane waved the question away and snorted. "Nah. They both needed a change a couple years ago, so I bought them out. You know, find their own way. The big city was calling."

Darcy slowly shook her head, studying him. "How do you manage it by yourself?"

"I'm good at delegating, I guess." He rested his ankle on the other knee. "No, seriously. I have a decent business manager. A good buddy from high school whom I'd trust with my firstborn. That and my parents still manage to poke their heads in every now and again to help out."

Her eyes widened. "Wait, did you just say 'firstborn'?"

"What? Yes...no!" Dane gritted his teeth and shook his head. "I shouldn't use baby metaphors."

She pressed a hand to her forehead. "You scared me. I thought I'd missed not only the birth announcement but a wedding too." She stopped, her eyes growing even larger. The word hung between them like a dead fish. "I'm sorry. I didn't mean to...to bring up weddings."

"It's fine. I'm over that. Water under the bridge as they say."

Darcy's expression was full of skepticism.

"I'm serious," he said.

Her brows pinched together as she gave him an earnest look. "Do you ever hear from her?"

"Never. She comes to town every now and again. Her parents still live there. I saw her coming out of the grocery store around Christmas. If she saw me, she didn't let on."

"That's too bad. I hate that your marriage ended like that. You're better off without her though. In hindsight, you know?"

Dane was silent. He didn't want to talk about his failed marriage to Felicia. He'd become pretty skilled at tamping those thoughts down into his mental trash compactor.

Darcy looked over her shoulder at the buffet table. "The line is short now. Time to grab a plate."

He slapped his knees before he got to his feet. "You don't have to tell me twice."

DANE GAZED AROUND THE TENT. THE LINE AT the buffet grew again after Darcy's husband put out the call for seconds. Pushing his plate away, he stood to stretch, again feeling the effects of not moving around as much as he was used to. Darcy still made the rounds among her guests and was now held hostage by Yandi and Meg at their table. He smiled as Darcy kept nodding, probably resigned to not getting a word in between them. That was quite the concession for Darcy. She was used to leading conversations.

He'd wanted to ask Darcy about Hilary. Dane doubted she'd offer anything he didn't already know, anything more than what he'd found out from Hilary on the two-hour ride back to Hendricks. And Darcy might take his questions as an opportunity to play matchmaker too. No, thanks. He'd been on the receiving end of one too many match attempts since he and Felicia imploded. Besides, what was the point? She wore a ring.

Hilary sat two tables away, poking at the food on her plate, wearing a polite-looking smile. Flanking her, Meg and Yandi were back to entertaining the whole table with their mother-daughter act. Their raucous laughter carried throughout the tent, earning smiles from people at the fringes of the crowd. Yet despite the happy sounds, Hilary hadn't looked up, hadn't talked to anyone at her table, or changed her expression from the frozen smile. What was it about her that made him unable to tear his eyes away? She was beautiful, yes. The downward slant to the corners of her eyes lent a sadness to them. But when she smiled, laugh lines framed her eyes and a dimple appeared high on each cheek. Her shoulders were drawn forward as if she might fold into herself if someone looked her way. Dane wondered why she was here when she so clearly looked like she wished she were someplace else.

He cleared his spot, walking the empty plate over to the garbage before he stopped at the bar. Dane ordered another whiskey sour, then he stood off to the side to watch the crowd. He should have been up in his room preparing for the keynote, but he'd had trouble wrapping his head around his presentation so far.

Hilary looked up, catching his eye. Dane smiled.

His heart jumped as she got up from the table with her half-filled plate and dumped it into the trash. When Dane realized she headed his way, he discreetly tucked his shirttail into his belt and squared his shoulders.

She gave him a quick, fleeting smile when she stopped next to him, a swish of her sweater brushing his arm.

"Hi there," she said. She crossed her arms and looked in toward the middle of the tent. Her voice was louder, more direct than it had been in the car.

"Are you feeling better?" Dane looked down at her. The string lights overhead made the top of her auburn head glow like a copper kettle.

Her face registered surprised. "How did you know?"

"I asked Darcy when I didn't see you on the bus for the Hendricks tour."

Another small smile. "Yes, I am. Traveling messes with my head."

There was more to it than that, he knew.

"Any more news from your sister-in-law?" Dane sipped his drink, wondering again if he was too intrusive with the questions. He already knew she liked her privacy.

"She's not coming after all."

"That's too bad."

"Her dad's been in the hospital."

"Will he be okay?"

"Yes, he will." Hilary uncrossed her arms and one hand flitted into the air dismissively. She turned slightly. "Anyway, thanks again for the ride today."

Was that what she'd crossed the tent to tell him? It felt a little anticlimactic. "You're welcome."

"I wasn't very talkative."

He almost nodded but caught himself.

A breeze snapped the tent flap behind them and they startled. He caught the scent of lavender from the table arrangements. Or was it her?

"Well, have a good night," Hilary said over her shoulder as she walked away.

He watched her cut across the lawn toward the house, hands clasped behind her back, taking her time. He could still see Hilary's silhouetted figure once she was inside the house until she disappeared farther into its depths.

"You too," he said to himself.

Chapter Five

H ilary didn't care for professional conferences.
When she'd worked in Canyon County
schools, she attended a few every year. People
tended to find their tribe within the first day, and that
never worked well for quiet types like her. The vibe
wasn't much different at this one. It didn't help that
she'd nursed her headache yesterday in her room while
everyone else was bused around town, making
connections. Small talk was hard enough when headaches
weren't part of the equation. She couldn't pretend to
listen when the only thing she could hear was the
pounding in her ears.

She was acutely aware of how alone she was as she sat
in the sunlit room downstairs in Blueberry Point Lodge
the next morning. She counted at least sixty people
seated at the round tables scattered around the room.

When the breakfast buffet opened at seven, she'd taken a plate back to her room to eat in peace, not thinking most seats would be filled before she returned for the start of the conference. It was her own fault. Going out of her way to not meet anyone cost her.

At the front of the room, Dane Porter wrapped up his keynote speech. With a projector screen on the wall behind him, Dane stood at the oak podium. He'd dazzled the group for the last forty minutes with anecdotes of running his lavender farm, making it sound way more captivating than Hilary imagined growing flowers could be. He was a livelier speaker than he let on yesterday during the car ride. Funny, actually. She liked how he gripped the podium after he told a joke like he expected the thing to topple from the force of his own laughter. He had one of those infectious laughs too. Not quite a giggle, but it rolled in his chest like he was full of bubbles.

So his farm was in Clove, Oregon. She'd never heard of the town, though she knew the area. It was east of Bend, which she'd passed through a few times. It was stunning in the fall. Clove was within a half day's drive from Redville. She and Will drove through that part of the state during their honeymoon six years ago.

"Can you imagine working on a flower farm? That's my dream," whispered the woman named Lucy Riggins sitting beside her. Hilary's short conversation with her before the welcome address revealed Lucy worked as a floral designer at the nursery in town.

"That's why we're here, right? To dream?" Hilary said.

"To turn dreams into reality actually," said the woman across the table who had been twisting her beaded cuff bracelets around her wrist since Hilary sat down. The constant rustling of beads was driving Hilary a little crazy. Lucy arched her brows at the woman's curt tone, then turned back to Hilary.

"I have a small plot south of town," Lucy continued. "My plan is to grow flowers for wholesale. I've already met with the bank."

It was hard not to respond to Lucy's excitement. Hilary loved her style too. The white sweater vest Lucy wore positively overwhelmed her, but she made it work with the mustard-colored velvet tunic underneath. That and the black Moto boots. Hilary could never pull it off. Besides, Jorie would laugh her off the farm.

Lucy noticed her coveting the vest. "Like it? It's alpaca. Letta Arbuckle is a master fiber artist in town." She craned her neck. "We'll probably see her this afternoon. I can introduce you."

"That's all right. I don't really dress up much. Basically, I live in flannel shirts and Wranglers."

Lucy twisted her hair and tossed the knot over one shoulder. She leaned toward Hilary, speaking under her breath. "It's not what you wear, but how you wear it."

Hilary laughed. Yes, she liked Lucy very much. Hilary guessed they were about the same age.

"What are you here for?" Lucy asked.

She'd been asked that question at least a dozen times since yesterday. Hilary practiced rehearsing an answer, even writing it down on the blank pad of paper with the Blueberry Point logo at the top she'd found on her nightstand. The words sounded clunky coming out of her mouth so she'd spent ten minutes working on a smoother response until she was happy.

"My sister-in-law and I hope to open a bed-and-breakfast and an apple orchard adjacent to our farm. We're exploring the working visitor concept." She cringed inwardly. *Way* too formal.

"I stayed at one of those once," Lucy said. "My parents thought we should do this working vacation thing one year. Too bad it was the rainiest year on record in Ohio." Lucy rolled her eyes. "It was awful. We didn't come prepared with enough clothes. Luckily, the couple had a son who was a year younger than me. My older sister and I borrowed some of his clothes while we mucked horse stalls and weeded the mother's flower garden in the rain."

Hilary chuckled. "That sounds memorable."

"We laugh about it now."

Hilary mimicked writing something down. "Note to self: Have used clothing on hand for unprepared guests."

"Yes!" Lucy opened her folder. "So, what's on the agenda today? Looks like an organic vegetable farm."

"We won't be mucking stalls at least," Hilary joked,

reading over her own agenda. DLA Northwoods Organix. Hoop houses. It sounded tame enough.

She'd huddled under the Egyptian cotton sheets earlier, reluctant to get up, and wondered again about her purpose here at the conference. Without Jorie, it felt like she wore someone else's shoes, a not-quite-right style in the wrong size. Jorie's enthusiasm for this dream of theirs carried Hilary. Sure, she was excited to take Larkin Farms in a new direction, but without Jorie, she lacked the drive to carry it.

"Anyway, the Arbuckles are nice people. They keep a really clean operation."

Lucy rattled on about the Arbuckles, but her voice faded as Dane walked away from the podium. Three people swarmed him immediately. He had a really nice smile. She liked how he hunched forward, always turning his ear to listen. So engaged.

"I'm going to head up to my room to change. I'll see you in a bit."

Lucy's words didn't register until she pushed away from the table. Hilary nodded and mumbled, "Okay," glancing at her when Lucy gathered her folder and coffee mug. Across the room, Dane dismissed himself from the group and walked toward her table. Hilary stood and smoothed the wrinkles from her top. She swept her notes and agenda into her folder. "Maybe I'll come too."

· · ·

THE AFTERNOON STOP WAS FORTY-FIVE MINUTES from Hendricks, up a winding, fir-lined highway. With Lake Superior behind them, Hilary had the chance to enjoy the different landscape through Finland State Forest. Tamaracks and spruce sheltered the forest floor, dropping shadows on a dark green canvas. Since vegetation had yet to reach its midsummer heights, granite outcrops popped out along the roadside. Farther in the woods, snow from a late-spring storm still stood in pillowy mounds where the sun hadn't reached to melt it.

Darcy's husband, Sean, drove while talking into the headset, sharing some local history about Hendricks and the area. Hilary listened as she stared out the window. Lucy was next to her, sketching in a journal. Two seats ahead, Dane sat by himself. The back of his head was a strange distraction. His hair had a subtle wave to it. Thick too. She bet it was almost long enough to gather into a hair tie. It took a certain kind of guy to pull off the look. Dane Porter would definitely fall into that category. Hilary mentally shook herself. What was she doing daydreaming about Dane's hair?

The bus pulled into the gravel drive. A wooden sign greeted them—DLA Northwoods Organix. Del Arbuckle, the owner and also an auctioneer in town, was a third-generation farmer, Sean explained before he parked the bus next to one of the tunnel-like hoop houses.

"He's quite the character, too, as you'll soon find out," Sean said as he opened the bus door.

Del Arbuckle had one hand on a fence post and his other wrapped around a pitchfork "to keep the *American Gothic* stereotype alive," he announced right away. A communal chuckle rose from his already captive audience. He squinted as they gathered around him, a coffee stirrer bobbing between his teeth. Sean introduced him while Del hung his head, nodding and huffing.

A dozen people raised their hands when Del asked if hoop houses were part of their vision. Next to her, Lucy thrust her hand into the air.

"I'm having two hoop houses built before next winter," she whispered to Hilary as she dropped her hand. "Del helped me order them. He's been a huge help."

Hilary wanted to step to the back of the group, but Lucy clutched her arm. "It's so nice to have connections. I can't imagine going through this alone."

Oof. Lucy didn't realize the impact of her words of course, but it squeezed Hilary's chest. Here she was without Jorie. The resentment she'd felt yesterday when Jorie said she'd stay behind still simmered. Hilary was out of her element. Trained in social work, for goodness' sake, not farming. But here she was, touring organic hoop houses and learning about fertilizer. She had enough trouble keeping her plants alive.

When the group followed Del into the first greenhouse, Hilary waited. Lucy walked on ahead, her eyes wide with excitement. She turned to say something, and Hilary saw her startle when she realized someone else was beside her instead of Hilary. She felt a nudge of guilt for escaping, but the constant activity of the day was starting to overwhelm her.

"You don't want to miss Del's narration of his beloved hoop houses. It's a top act, I hear."

The voice in her ear raised the hair on the back of her neck.

Dane.

"I've heard that too."

The words flew out of Hilary's mouth before she comprehended their meaning. Her brain was mush. What had she heard? What did that mean?

Dane stood shoulder to shoulder with her. "We have some hoop houses back home. Our winters are relatively mild though."

That thing inside her head—a gray blob. She'd lost her ability to speak.

Dane leaned toward her as they followed the small group ahead of them. "I can't imagine apple orchards do very well in hoop houses."

Okay, that was a joke. She recognized the humor in his tone. Plus, he grinned when he said it. Faith in her senses—at least her humor-detection one—was restored. Did she already tell Dane about their business plan? She didn't remember revealing that much to him.

She laughed. "They probably don't come in extra large, do they?"

He paused for a second, looking at her. His forehead wrinkled like he didn't get it. But then his face lit up and he was gracious enough to chuckle. "If they did I'm—"

Bam!

She saw it coming at the last second and couldn't warn him fast enough. Dane's forehead met the corner of a rolling metal rack that he didn't see as he walked beside her, veering into the thing on accident. It wobbled, threatening to fall onto him as he bent at the waist, but she caught it, setting it upright. She laid a hand across Dane's back as he covered his forehead with one hand, resting the other on his knee. He groaned.

"Oh, Dane. Are you all right?" Hilary asked. It was a stupid question. Of course he wasn't all right. The man crashed head-on into stainless steel. Hilary looked up as a few stragglers double-backed to check on him too.

"Better ask the rack. I'm sure it took the brunt of it," he said, straightening. He pressed gingerly on the spot along his hairline. Blood wet his fingers when he took his hand away.

Del heard the commotion and hobbled back to the end of the line. "What happened?"

Dane's face flamed. "It's totally my fault. I need to keep an eye on what's ahead of me instead of what's beside me apparently." He didn't look at her, but Hilary caught his meaning.

"That's not going to improve your looks any," Del said with all the seriousness of an accountant in April.

Dane snorted and gave him a small grin. "Funny."

Del hooked his hands in his pockets and leaned back slightly, studying Dane's forehead. The older man was a good six inches shorter than Dane. He pointed his thumb over his shoulder toward Sean, who jogged toward the tour bus. "Sean is preparing for surgery now. Can you see straight?"

"I don't wear glasses if that's what you mean," Dane said hesitantly.

"No, I mean now after you almost killed my rack."

"Oh." Dane turned and squinted toward Hilary. "Yes, everything looks good."

Hilary hid her smile as she dipped her head.

Del took an orange bandana from his pocket and swiped it across his own forehead. "Good. I can't afford to be sued."

Hilary exchanged a look with Dane. He took it more in stride than she would if it were her forehead. Del's dry sense of humor didn't seem very appropriate at the moment.

Sean returned from the bus with a first aid kit. He set it on a nearby table and popped the lid. "We'll get you cleaned up," he said.

"Really, it's a scratch," Dane said, chuckling. He gritted his teeth when Sean pressed an antiseptic wipe on the now present lump.

Hilary watched his expression for signs that the knock was more than a superficial scratch. Dane seemed more embarrassed than injured. He avoided looking at her, even blushing a little when Sean peeled the bandage from its wrapper and applied it to Dane's head.

Del ambled away to continue the tour while Sean finished treating Dane. Sean gave him another antiseptic wipe for the blood on his fingers. Hilary tried to gauge how much pain Dane was in but his expression was stoic. With a square of gauze now in place, Dane pressed his finger to the spot.

"Good as new," he said with a tentative smile.

"Maybe you should sit for a while to make sure you're all right." She almost caught his arm when he wobbled next to her until she realized he'd stepped in a low spot on the lawn.

"No worries. It'll fade by tomorrow." He grimaced as his boots sank into the soggy ground. Hilary sidestepped a shallow puddle.

She laughed, looking at him in disbelief. "I don't think so. It's a good-sized gash. Don't be so cavalier."

It was Dane's turn to laugh, the corners of his eyes crinkling in a mischievously boyish way. He seemed to like playing with her. "And don't distract me with big words. I should know my own head anyway."

Hilary didn't want to fuss over him; she barely knew him. But he really took a hit, and those head injuries could be tricky, the effects not seen until hours later. "I'm trying to help. Sorry for…caring."

His smile faded and he slowed. He must have realized

she was serious. "No, I'm sorry. I'm making jokes, and you're trying to be considerate."

Sorry for caring.

It was an awkward thing to say. Her mouth ran away from her brain when her guard was down; it had always been a problem. But Dane went out of his way to make comfortable since the ride back to Hendricks yesterday and she fell for it. His attentiveness breached the wall she'd built around herself. He asked questions and then listened. It was a little unnerving, having his full attention. She needed to watch herself.

"No worries." She gave him what she hoped was a neutral smile. "If you're sure you're okay, I'm going to catch up with the others. I've already missed enough."

She hurried away, craning her neck to look for Lucy. She spotted Lucy's alpaca vest near the front and skirted the group to catch up to her. She'd learned a lesson from Dane—talk less and listen more. And try to steer clear of overly friendly conference presenters with soulful eyes.

Chapter Six

T hat night Dane fumbled for the light switch in his room. The overhead light blinked on, temporarily blinding him. He studied his bare feet behind half-closed lids before he adjusted to the bright room. It was after midnight. The pain reliever Darcy offered him earlier had worn off. He never took painkillers so she'd had a hard time convincing him to take the darned things. But the bump on his head throbbed now, keeping him from falling back asleep.

He should have taken the bottle when she pressed it into his hand. "You'll need more, trust me," she said. He'd laughed. Meds were for wimps. But oh how he wished for them now. Dane could deal with pain. It was the sleep he couldn't live without. He was used to his schedule back home. In bed by ten, up at five. A solid seven hours—uninterrupted since he slept like a rock—

suited him. Anything less made him grumpy. Caffeine couldn't even work its magic when he was too sleep-deprived.

The downside of staying in one of the private guest cabins on the property was the short but cold walk he'd have to make across the lawn to the inn. The bottle sat on the kitchen counter where he'd left it. He slipped into his boots, threw on his coat, and stepped onto the porch.

It was a clear, cold night. His breath huffed out in a cloud as he gazed at the three-quarter moon keeping company with the scattered stars. The inn was dark except for a couple lights left on in the rooms of the main floor. The patio light was on too.

Dane used the code to open the back door, careful not to make a sound. Inside, he left his boots on the mat and padded across the living room, weaving between the tables set up for the conference. In the foyer, he turned left and followed the hall down to the commercial-sized kitchen. A small light above the stove illuminated the countertops and he quickly found the bottle. Sweet relief.

He was looking through the cabinets for water glasses when he heard a floorboard creak. Old houses were full of noises. He should know; he lived in one. Change in the seasonal temperatures had a way of making old houses talk, even one this solid. He opened nearly half the cabinets in the kitchen when he found the glassware. He turned on the faucet, filling the glass, when a more distinct creak caught his attention again.

"I thought I was the only night owl around here."

He almost dropped the glass.

It was Hilary, leaning against the doorframe in a rosy-hued robe, her hair tousled around her face like she'd been having as much trouble as he'd had falling asleep. Dane swallowed hard.

"I'm not really a night owl. This is keeping me up." He pointed to the lump on his forehead.

She came toward him slowly, squinting to see it in the dim light. "Hurts, doesn't it? And you were so insistent it was nothing." In the near dark, her eyes were hooded, giving them a seductive light.

"Masculine pride has to count for something."

"Yeah, something foolish." Hilary laughed. "I've never understood it. What's the point of pretending you're not hurt, even as blood seeps through your fingers?"

"Now that you put it like that…"

Hilary nodded slowly, the smile still there.

He downed two tablets, took a drink, and refilled the glass with tap water. "So what are you doing down here?"

"I came for some tea. Join me?"

He was a coffee man. Two cups a day, three during harvest. He'd never tried tea. Now was not the time to admit it. "Sure, why not?"

There was a serving cart in the corner with a coffee maker, mugs, and enough single-serve coffees, packets of hot chocolate and cider, and boxes of tea to keep the entire town satisfied from now until Christmas. Hilary set two mugs on the counter and took her time studying the tea varieties.

She held a finger up, her focus still on the cart. "Don't tell me—an herbal blend, right?"

"How'd you guess?"

"You own a lavender farm."

Dane slid a stool away from the center island and sat down. "That's really brilliant."

Hilary tapped her temple when she turned around, then went back to heating water in the coffee maker. He grinned

A few minutes later she set two mugs down on the island. She pulled out another stool and sat across from him. She dipped her tea bag into the water, draping the string thing over the side. Okay, that was simple.

Elbows on the counter, she clutched the mug with both hands. Dane waited for her to say something, but she seemed content with the silence for now. Somewhere in the house, a door closed. He sipped the tea, struggling to keep a grimace off his face. He couldn't believe people actually enjoyed this stuff.

"I never told you how much I liked your keynote," Hilary said, finally looking up at him. "You really had them laughing."

"Never realized how funny lavender farming could be, did you?"

Her smile widened. "Not for a minute."

"I figured if the subject matter bored them I can at least disguise it with humor." He shrugged.

"Good strategy." She picked up the spoon and stirred her tea. "Did you always know you wanted to work on your family's farm as a career?"

"Honestly? I didn't think about it until my uncle passed away ten years ago. He and my dad farmed it together. But it felt pretty natural stepping into his role after I got out of the navy." He'd been too carefree as a teen to look to the future. Working alongside his father and uncle were so routine he never regarded it as a career, only a way to keep a few bucks in his wallet. But then Uncle Chuck had a heart attack. A bad one. He raised a can of cola to his lips one July afternoon and never took that sip. Dane's father took Uncle Chuck's death especially hard. They'd been the best of friends as well as brothers.

Hilary blew into her cup. "It must smell heavenly, the farm when it's in bloom," she mused while she dipped her spoon into the cup, playing with the tea bag.

"It does."

"Lavender always reminds me of the sachets my grandma used to keep in her chest of drawers. She used to rub oil on my wrists before bedtime when I stayed at her house. Said it would help me sleep." She closed her eyes for a moment as if watching a film play out in her head. "Good memories."

"That's true. It's also good for stress and anxiety. Oil in our shop sells out quite a bit."

The look she gave him made him think he'd hit a nerve. He took another sip of tea and shuddered.

"What other good memories do you have?" He was stepping into sensitive territory he knew, but he wanted to steer the conversation away from negative thoughts. She'd shied away before from answering too many questions. Maybe the quiet house, the tea, and the dimly lit kitchen empowered him.

Hilary rested her chin in her hand. "Oh, let's see," she said wistfully. "Summer vacations on Puget Sound, a yellow barn cat I named Arrabelle, my mother's cranberry apple pie."

"Your mom is a good baker?" Dessert was always a happy topic.

"A *phenomenal* baker. She's the pastry manager at a restaurant in Napa. I think I even remember a recipe for lavender apple pie in her pie bible."

"A pie bible? She *is* one serious baker."

Hilary laughed. "It sounds intense, but trust me, if you tasted one of her pies, you'd understand. She replicated the book for my sister and me. We each have our own copy."

"Lavender apple pie, huh?"

Hilary nodded and sipped her tea. "I've never tried it. Maybe I should experiment when I get home. You can send me some lavender."

"So will baking pies fit into the apple orchard venture somehow?"

She looked at her mug, lifting it to her lips. "Yes, I suppose so," she said before she sipped.

Her tone was noncommittal as it was each time he'd asked her something about her business plan. So far, she'd deferred to her sister-in-law, saying "Jorie's taking care of that" or given him a trite response before changing the subject. Hilary had yet to show any real passion for their project. He wondered if coming to this conference had been her idea or her sister-in-law's.

"I've shared enough. It's your turn," she said.

"Good memories?" He tapped his spoon on the counter, thinking. "Well, here's one: Hurricane Katrina."

Her mug froze in midair. The corners of her mouth turned down. "Uh, that's a rather odd good memory."

"It didn't quite come out the way I intended. It was a *transformative* memory for me. How's that?"

"Better."

"Anyway, our church took a mission trip down there after it happened. I was in my late teens at the time. There was a group of fifteen of us. We basically worked on houses, cleaning them out, doing repairs, making them habitable again."

"I can't even imagine what the conditions were like in those places."

"Some houses had water up to the top of the doorframe. Mold. And critters like you couldn't imagine."

Hilary shuddered. "Don't say any more. I'll trust you on that."

Dane chuckled. "Fair enough."

"That must have been satisfying, though. Seeing the progress. Having a hand in it."

"It was. But even more than that it showed those people they weren't forgotten. I think having strangers work on your behalf when you're at rock bottom is so powerful. It made a lasting impression on me, at least."

"I get it. It's why I loved being a school social worker."

Dane cupped his mug, pausing to let that new bit of information seep in. "So, you're not anymore?"

She shook her head, not looking up. "No. I lost my job when my school district consolidated with another."

"What did you love about it?"

Hilary's grin spread across her face. "Definitely the kids. Junior high kids get such a bad rap, but I adored them. I really felt I'd found my calling."

"Maybe you'll find something else someday?"

"Probably not." Hilary hitched a shoulder. "Now Jorie has this idea... I mean, Jorie and I are going into business together, so it's just as well."

They sat there in the stillness, Hilary sipping her tea while he pretended to. He glanced at the clock on the wall. A half hour had passed.

"I'm getting sleepy. Finally." Hilary rubbed the back of her neck.

"Happy to have sufficiently bored you."

She giggled. "No, it was the tea." She glanced at his nearly full mug. "How was yours?"

"Truth? I don't like tea."

Hilary wrinkled her nose. "I can tell."

"How?" He pushed his mug away. It tasted like warm, perfumed water.

"You didn't let it steep at all." She took one last sip, hiding a smile behind the mug.

"Now you probably think I was trying to impress you or something." He watched the dimples at the tops of her cheeks appear.

"Or something," she said, laughter in her voice.

Their eyes locked. For a moment, Dane felt the draw of some invisible force pulling him closer to her. Or trying to anyway. The kitchen island separated them by three feet. Three agonizing feet.

"What do you think that something might be?" He kept his tone light. Dane couldn't tear his eyes away from hers. Half of Hilary's face was lit by the stove lamp, the other half shrouded in shadows. She was beyond beautiful.

"I'm too tired to guess," she said softly, taking their mugs to the sink. When she turned to him, her eyes were sleepy. She blinked lazily as she pulled her robe tight around her neck again. The ring on her finger flashed from the light above the stove.

"Good night, Dane," she said.

"Sweet dreams. Better luck this time."

Dane sat in the kitchen for several minutes, listening to the sound of her footsteps on the stairs. He listened for the soft click of her door and anything else that might give him a mental image before she slipped into bed again. His head was filled with thoughts he hadn't entertained in a while. A long while. They stirred him and he caught himself smiling. That wall she'd built around herself still stood. But after tonight, he'd finally been able to peer over the top to what lie beyond. And Dane liked what he saw.

This midnight talk with Hilary also brought an unpleasant memory to the forefront again—his disastrously short marriage. Dane kept that one tucked away; he preferred it that way. But sometimes it snuck up on him, especially when he entertained the notion that maybe there was someone else out there for him.

When he found out Felicia cheated on him the night before their wedding three years ago, he was crushed like he'd never been before. He learned of the hookup a week later in the middle of their Alaskan honeymoon. His best man called to tell him one of the groomsmen, a guy Dane had known since grade school, got together with Felicia after the wedding party left the rehearsal dinner. Dane immediately confronted Felicia on the deck of their cruise ship with Dawes Glacier in the background. It took months for the anger and humiliation to subside and even longer before he could muster the mental energy to write heartfelt notes to send along with the gifts he returned to their guests. The marriage was annulled, Felicia moved to Bend, and he resumed life on the farm as a single man. It was far from the ideal life he'd envisioned for himself at age twenty-eight.

In the months after his marriage ended, he questioned himself. How had she blindsided him so easily? Dane wondered how he could be such a poor judge of character. He'd known Felicia since high school. She was class president and a captain of the volleyball team, a real go-getter even though her family moved to the area when she was a teen. During her four years at Oregon State, they stayed in touch, seeing each other once a month when she came back to Clove since their friend circles intertwined. Then one weekend in February, three years after she'd graduated college, a freak snowstorm stranded Dane, Felicia, and six of their mutual friends at the Lake Randolph Ski Resort. It forced them to add an extra two days to what was supposed to be an overnight trip. There, Dane got to know Felicia. Really know her. She loved her work with a nonprofit, dreamed of working in the Peace Corps, and was a fitness fanatic who coached others through home tutorials in her spare time. When he looked back, he saw their goals didn't align at all. He'd been drawn to her ambition. What he didn't see was her restlessness, a need to be involved in the next new thing. That wouldn't have mixed well with his lifestyle. He was Dane Porter, owner of Lavender Lane Farm in Clove,

Oregon, and would be for the rest of his life if he were lucky.

Dane slid the stool under the counter and walked through the darkened house. He slipped his boots back on, careful not to lose his balance and clatter into the door or an end table or a piece of lint on the rug. He was beyond clumsy sometimes, hence the lump on his head.

He chuckled as he let himself out of the house. No, the lump on his head happened because he'd been distracted. Sweetly distracted, but distracted all the same.

Chapter Seven

It was well past two o'clock when Hilary finally drifted off to sleep. She slept so solidly that her phone alarm failed to wake her the next morning. It was the sun slicing through the curtains that finally made her stir at a quarter to eight. She popped up, fearing breakfast was over, but was relieved when she heard people outside her door heading downstairs.

Today she was determined to sit in the dining room and eat breakfast with everyone else. No more hiding in her room. It was strange, but she felt a sense of renewed purpose for being there. Maybe she was meant to come to the conference after all, with or without Jorie. She didn't want to disappoint her sister-in-law anyway. Jorie was right. Opening the B & B would honor Will's dream for Larkin Farms. Well, *her* dream too.

In the conference room, a handful of people stood at

the buffet. The room was bright and airy, the tall windows revealing another clear day outside. The lake looked calm. There was a ship in the distance, and gulls flew along the shore in perfect synchronicity. Hilary made her way over to the food and lifted the lid on the first serving pan. An egg scramble with peppers, sausage, and cheese. It looked amazing. The light dinner she'd eaten last night was evident now in the way her mouth watered.

Lucy sidled up alongside her.

"Good morning. I wondered if you'd taken breakfast upstairs again when I didn't see you."

Her tone was like a song sparrow's, bright and trilling. Lucy wore another eclectic outfit. A tiny black accordion-pleated blouse and wide-legged red pants. The black Moto boots finished it off again. The outfit was more appropriate for a bridal shower, not stomping around gardens. The girl had fashion guts, that was for sure.

"No, I slept in. I guess this Northwoods air makes me extra sleepy." Hilary moved along the line to make room for her.

"Did you hear that wind this morning? It was crazy."

She must have slept solid. Hilary hadn't heard a thing. "No, not at all."

"I thought the house would blow off its foundation." Lucy took a plate from the stack and scooped out some scrambled eggs. "I love that top, by the way. It really says spring to me."

"Thank you."

Hilary glanced down at herself momentarily as she set the lid down on the serving pan. She'd intended to save the top for the closing event on the last night of the conference. It was way fancier than what she usually wore now that she didn't work outside the home. The woman in Claret's back home said the dark green floral pattern really complemented her hair and eyes. Hilary especially loved the almost sheer sleeves. It was feminine without being fussy, and it suited her mood today.

Hilary finished filling her plate and searched the room for a place to sit. Empty spots at tables nearby tempted her. She should learn the art of small talk if hosting guests was in her future. But an empty table by the window with a view of the lake won her over. She hurried between the tables and set her plate down, claiming it before another introvert beat her to it. She'd practice making small talk some other time. Besides, she was starving, and eating while talking wasn't going to make her any friends. Hilary scooped up a spoonful of egg.

"I had my eye on this exact spot. Great minds and all that."

She didn't have to look behind her to know who the voice belonged to. Her egg fell from her spoon, scattering on the tablecloth around her plate.

Dane pulled the chair away and set his plate down, which was heaped to the rim.

"You look rested. That tea must have done the trick," he said.

She reloaded her spoon, scooping up half the amount she'd spilled.

"It did. Always does." Hilary brought the napkin to her mouth while she chewed. "It must have worked for you too. Oh wait, you're not a tea drinker." She hid her smile behind the napkin, glancing at him.

Dane grinned. He was a good-looking guy when he wasn't smiling. She couldn't help but notice it on Sunday when she saw him for the first time at the airport. But here in the sunny room, the laugh lines around his eyes and his reddened cheeks from spending most of the afternoon outside yesterday at Del's farm were on full display. It added to his charm. Hilary looked away quickly when she realized she'd been staring.

"Very funny," he said. "I was just thinking how nice it was to talk to you last night. Now I realize it only gave you ammunition to pick on me."

She giggled. "You have to be careful these days."

His gaze raked over her while she chewed. She focused on her breakfast, pushing egg around on her plate. Maybe she should have taken the meal in her room after all. If she ate any slower, it'd be time for lunch before she finished. Why wasn't he eating?

"I was thinking about what you said last night," he said, finally picking up his fork. "About your mother's pies."

"Oh?"

"Have you thought about selling pies and other apple-based goods? If your mother is that good of a baker—"

"The best."

"I'm sure she is," he said with a small smile. "I wasn't questioning her skills."

"Sorry." Hilary set her fork down and took a deep breath. His closeness made her so self-conscious.

"The pie bible of hers might mean you're sitting on a gold mine."

"So, what are you saying?"

"You have an apple orchard that isn't being used. There would be hardly any overhead. And your mother is a professional baker."

"That doesn't mean she passed her talent to me."

Dane gave her a skeptical look. "C'mon. You told me last night you're the family dessert czar."

"Czarina."

"Is that what you call a female czar? Sorry, I erred on the side of caution."

She chuckled. "I did say that, didn't I?"

His grin broadened. "You did."

"It was one o'clock in the morning. People tell a lot of untruths at that hour of the night."

Dane propped an elbow on the table, resting his cheek in his hand. "Really?"

She nodded. "All the time."

They stared at each other for a few seconds too long.

A shiver ran through Hilary. Her face grew hot and she looked down at her plate. She laughed again.

"I've forgotten where we were going with this."

The spell broken, Dane reached for his coffee.

"Profit margins," he said, shrugging. "You have an apple orchard. I think you should use it."

B & B's. Apple orchards. Overhead and profit margins. It all made her head spin. Why couldn't Jorie have come?

"I don't think we intend to do anything more than offer a u-pick option." The discomfort she felt even talking about the business side of Larkin Farms was probably written all over her face. Her ignorance about its operation was so obvious.

"Really? Seems like a lot of trouble taking care of trees if you don't capitalize on them."

"Maybe someday. It depends on what Jorie wants to do."

Dane paused. "You defer to her a lot," he said, cocking his head, looking at her through one eye.

"I do? I guess because she has the business experience and, well, I don't."

Hilary never felt she and Jorie were anything but equal partners in this venture though. They each had their gifts. Jorie's expertise lie in keeping the books. Her talents lie in stripping wallpapers and refinishing woodwork, anything that didn't involve actual construction. Converting the farmhouse into a place for guests was a larger project than they anticipated. If anything, Hilary had been the one to coordinate a schedule for renovations and do much of the manual labor herself. It was a welcome distraction when grief over Will's death threatened to monopolize her thoughts.

But she and Jorie soon found out it would need more work—major work. The foundation near the kitchen was crumbling, something that wasn't apparent until the evergreen bushes were cut back last summer. Work slowed to a crawl since foundation work hadn't figured into the budget. Yet Hilary's optimism for keeping the dream alive—Will's dream—never wavered. Not until this week, anyway, when she started questioning herself. And now Dane pointed out her dependence on Jorie.

Dane continued, concentrating on his mound of hash browns. "There's nothing wrong with not being comfortable managing the books. My dad always looked to his brother in business matters, not wanting to be bothered. It wasn't his strength."

"I can relate."

He pointed to her hand with his fork. "Is your husband involved with the plans?"

It was such a casual question, an extension of their conversation, which flowed so easily that she shook her head before it registered what he'd asked. Hilary held her breath. She set the spoon on her plate. Across the table, Lucy chatted with an older woman wearing a "Keep Calm and Farm On" tee shirt, oblivious to her and Dane.

She stared at the ring on her left hand. It usually

resided on the other hand where it had been for the last year. For some reason she'd moved it back to her other ring finger during the flight to Duluth. She could think of no reasonable explanation for why she did it. Honestly, she hadn't given the ring another thought until now. Hilary tucked her hand into her lap and swallowed.

"No," she said. "He's not."

Dane's fork froze in midair as he stared at her. His expression was neutral, but Hilary could read the questions behind his blank look. He cleared his throat, turning his attention back to the breakfast in front of him.

"Well, it sounds like Jorie is a godsend then," he said brightly. Dane flipped open his folder as he dug into his breakfast again. "So, what's on the agenda today?"

Hilary slowly exhaled. Dane's attention was drawn away from her at the moment. Her pulse thudded in her throat. She swallowed again and opened her folder. While she was thankful he didn't press the question about Will, the awkwardness still blazed across her skin.

Dane tapped his finger on the agenda. "Look at that. 'Writing a Business Plan' is the first topic. Sounds like it's right up your alley," he said, nodding. "Too bad your business manager will miss it."

For the first time that day, she wished Jorie was sitting next to her. Hilary looked at the time on her phone: eight thirty. It'd taken her all of two hours for that thought to cross her mind. An improvement, for sure.

Chapter Eight

❦

When Darcy asked him to present at the conference, she'd mentioned a decent stipend as well as travel expenses. Dane jumped at the chance. Even though it meant leaving for a few days amidst a busy time of year, he could use the break. She'd also offered an even higher sum if he'd lend his expertise in another area: guiding her and Sean's project of irrigating their flower and herb garden with rainwater runoff. If there was anything he knew, it was irrigation. He'd designed a system for his vegetable garden with the runoff from the barn. Then he'd posted pictures on social media and before he knew it, a few of his friends asked for help with their projects. It had become a pretty good side gig in the off-season. Nothing too high-end, but it was labor intensive, which scared many from taking it on as a DIY job.

Dane took the afternoon off from the Bonnie Acres Bee Farm tour to get a closer look at the project. He'd left Hilary's side after the business planning seminar to join another group so they could pick his brain. He caught her staring at him from across the room a few times. Two days ago that would have thrilled him. He'd felt drawn to her since they'd talked in the car on Sunday. Her subtle wit and low-key manner captivated him. She seemed grounded, if not a little aloof, but he sensed an underlying warmth that few people probably had the privilege of realizing.

But that ring.

It was a glaring reminder that she was taken. And when he'd asked about her husband at breakfast, her mood shifted like mercury. She'd talked about Jorie's involvement back home, but made no mention of her husband. So he'd left that one question hanging in the air even though she'd barely whispered an answer. Something wasn't right.

After the conference group left in the two buses, Darcy helped Dane haul coils of garden hose from the shed near the back of the property. The temperature cooled off since the clouds rolled in. A little breeze ruffled the decaying leaves gathering in small piles against the building, remnants from last fall.

"What do you think of the conference so far?" asked Darcy as she dropped one of the bulky coils at her feet.

"I think it's fantastic. A good mixture of breakout topics and speakers. And the food—"

Darcy laughed. "I knew you'd say that."

"Seriously, I wasn't expecting people to come from around the country." He snipped the plastic ties holding the hose together, then passed the clippers to Darcy so she could do the same for the coils near her. "I figured it would only be regional folks."

"We were pretty lucky with the local businesses in the area. Once I put out the word that I needed sponsors, speakers, and demo farms, they came to me with people who wanted to take part." Darcy shrugged. "I didn't have to do any marketing other than open my big mouth at an economic development meeting last summer."

Dane chuckled. "You're pretty good at that, aren't you? Opening your big mouth."

"Some things never change. I wasn't elected cheerleading captain in high school for being a church mouse."

"So you're planning to go bigger next year?"

"That's the plan, though I don't know how we're going to squeeze anyone else in here or at the motel in town."

Dane thought of Hilary and her B & B dream. Too bad she wasn't local. He'd love to shoot some business her way. "Short-term housing might be your only option. Maybe some Airbnb folks could help with lodging."

"Yeah, I've thought of that." She stood upright,

stretching her back. "Sean and I need to open another lodge I guess."

Dane snorted. "What, you don't have your hands busy enough with this place?"

They walked over to the barn, dragging the ends of the hoses where three sixty-gallon rain barrels sat alongside the back wall.

"What's one more inn?" she joked. "I think one of our attendees has plans to offer lodging on her farm."

"Yes, Hilary Larkin and her sister, Jorie. Jorie is the one who missed her flight and decided not to come."

"I keep forgetting to check in with Hilary, see if she has any questions specific to innkeeping." Darcy gave him the side-eye. "I've seen you with Hilary more than once during the last two days. Did you two find some things in common?"

His first reaction to Darcy's observation was to deny it. He hadn't come to the conference to connect with anyone. It felt opportunistic, like he was trolling for a hookup. That was so out of character for him, even before he dated Felicia. But Darcy knew that about him. He didn't need to shy away from her question.

"She's fun to talk to."

Darcy nodded. "And very pretty."

He smiled, not looking at her. "That too."

Dane threaded the first hose onto the spigot near the bottom of the barrel. "She seems a little unsure of herself, like she's at a crossroads."

"Hopefully what she learns here can help her with that."

"I've been giving her a little direction."

"Uh-huh," said Darcy. "I'm sure you have."

"No, not like that. Anyway, she's married."

Darcy stopped twisting the hose onto the spigot of the second barrel. "That's too bad."

"Yeah, well. It's just my luck."

She cast him a sympathetic look. "There's someone out there for you, Dane. Don't let one bad apple rot the whole barrel."

Dane chuckled. "No worries. It'll happen when it happens."

THE TOUR BUSES RETURNED THREE HOURS later. He and Darcy finished up forty-five minutes earlier and were enjoying lemonades on the patio. They watched the group disembark from the buses, noticeably slower than when they'd left at lunchtime.

"Looks like they're all ready for a collective nap or something." Darcy rose to greet everyone while Dane drained his glass.

Dane sought out the olive-green coat with the Larkin Farms logo on the back. She was easy to spot with that spill of chestnut hair. That, and she was limping.

He set his glass on the side table and hurried to catch up to them as the group filed into the inn.

"Hilary."

She turned to him. The afternoon spent outside had whipped her hair into disheveled waves and pinkened her cheeks. Man, she was pretty. He pushed the thought aside as quickly as it popped into his head.

Dane nodded to her feet. "What happened?"

Hilary lifted her foot, and he immediately saw the problem. Her boot's sole had split, part of it missing. She took the piece from her jacket pocket. "I should have bought new ones before I came. This is what I get for being frugal."

"I understand the attachment to a good pair of boots. It's hard to let go sometimes."

Her eyes were wide as she nodded like she couldn't tell if he was joking. "The only other pair of shoes I brought is more appropriate for a business meeting than mucking around the countryside."

"There's an outfitter in town." Dane knew because he'd bought some repellant there on Sunday. "I could take you."

"I doubt they'd have the boots I like." She wrinkled her nose. "Creature of habit. Someone mentioned a general store though. Maybe I can pick up a cheap pair of athletic shoes."

Sean caught Darcy's eye. She gave him a knowing look, a one-sided smile lighting her eyes before she followed the others inside. He looked back at Hilary. "If that's what you want."

"Do you think the Stetmans will let you borrow their car again?" she said in a low voice.

Of course Darcy would let him take the car. The question was should he suggest she drive herself?

"I'll ask her."

"You don't mind driving me, do you?"

"I don't have anything better to do," he said, cursing to himself. *You like torturing yourself, don't you?*

Hilary stuffed the broken piece of sole back into her pocket. "Let me grab some things and I'll meet you back here in two minutes."

Twenty minutes later they pulled into a parking spot in front of Maisy Day's General Emporium in downtown Hendricks.

"I love this town," Hilary said, twisting in her seat to look behind them and across the street. "They've got a bakery and an ice cream shop in the same block? I could live here."

"We have a bakery in Clove. A darned good one."

"I have to drive ten miles to the nearest bakery where I'm from," she said.

"All the more reason you should use those apples to sell pie. You'll have a corner on the market."

She pursed her lips. "You're relentless when you take hold of an idea."

"Only good ideas."

Hilary dismissed the comment with a wave of her

hand. "Here's a better idea. We should get ice cream after I find shoes."

He gripped the steering wheel, staring straight ahead. Him and his brilliant ideas. Driving Hilary around town was decidedly not one of his better ones.

"Okay."

She gaped at him. "What, you don't like ice cream?"

"I love ice cream."

"Good, because I'm in the mood," she said, peering out her window at the front of the store. "This shouldn't take long. You can wait here if you'd like."

Dane sat there for a few seconds, wondering what he was doing. Didn't he give himself a lecture earlier about steering clear? And here he'd turned right around and jumped at the chance to drive her around the North Shore for shoes and ice cream. His willpower could use some work.

He unbuckled his belt. "No, I'll come in and check it out. I'm curious about what an emporium sells anyway."

Inside, a woman with hair like spun sugar bent over the front counter, working a crossword puzzle. She asked if she could help them while barely tearing her attention away from the puzzle. When Hilary said she wanted shoes, the woman pointed to the aisle in front of them with her pencil.

The store had a claustrophobic atmosphere. Long, narrow aisles and shelves were so tall they blocked the light from the fixtures overhead, bathing much of the merchandise in shadows. It was impossible for him and Hilary to walk side by side. Dane turned sideways to squeeze past a woman and her young son coming the opposite way.

"I've never seen so much…stuff," whispered Hilary as they walked toward the rear of the store. At the end of the aisle, she stopped in front of stacks of shoeboxes. None of the shoes were on display. Instead, Hilary squinted to see the black-and-white sketches on the end of each box.

Dane slid a box from the shelf and opened it. "It doesn't look like there's much of a selection."

"I'm not picky."

She peeked inside the box he held out and wrinkled her nose. Dane put it back on the shelf, smiling.

"Are you sure you don't want to try the outfitter?"

Hilary opened another box. "And pay five times the amount for a boot that isn't exactly what I want? No, thanks."

"You sure are budget-conscious for someone who insists she doesn't have a head for business." Dane opened another box. "How about this one?"

She put her box back on the shelf and looked at his. "I could live with those. I need a size eight." Hilary walked over to the chair against the back wall, waiting for him to find her size. "It's because I'm not good with bookkeeping that I need to be extra careful with my money."

He took the shoes from the box. "Okay, I get it."

Hilary slipped out of her boots to try the navy-blue athletic shoes. Dane squatted in front of her, slapping his knee so she'd put her foot up for him to tie the laces. She watched him with her hands in her lap.

"Tell me more about where you live," she asked finally. "There's a bakery and a lavender farm. What else does Clove have to offer?"

Dane glanced up. Her look was earnest, but there was a teasing lilt to her voice.

He concentrated on tying her shoe. "The town itself is very small but has a fun, laid-back vibe. Good leadership has brought in a few businesses, which have become destination shopping places—an outfitter, a farm-to-table restaurant, a few other things."

"That sounds a little like Ulander, though it's ten miles from our place. But it's the closest town."

"There's also the state forest adjacent to our land, so lots of recreation—hiking, biking, fishing. Our farm sits in a valley, but we're surrounded by hills."

"Hmm, sounds ideal."

Dane smiled. "It's home."

Hilary leaned back against the wall. "So do you have someone special back there? You know, a girlfriend?"

The loops he'd made with the laces weren't nearly as tight as they could be. He pulled on them, releasing the knot to start over. "Not at the moment." The sudden shift in topics surprised him. He wouldn't mind moving on to another subject just as quickly.

"But there was." It wasn't a question.

He took his time answering. Did he suddenly grow an extra set of fingers on each hand? He was having the darnedest time tying the laces.

"It's been a while."

She nudged his hand away, taking the laces. "That's really loose. Here, let me," Hilary said, bending over her shoes. She'd retied them in no time, popping up to pace the floor, testing the fit.

Dane used the break in conversation to wander into the next aisle. Looking at auto air fresheners seemed safer than revealing more about his relationship status. The more he talked with Hilary, the more his attraction grew. Aside from questions about his love life, they talked easily, drifting from one subject into the next like they hadn't met days ago. It had been like that the night before in the kitchen and this afternoon on the way to town. They hadn't stopped talking since he pulled out of the driveway at Blueberry Point Lodge.

But that darned ring. They could talk until his voice grew hoarse, but it wouldn't change the fact she was married.

Chapter Nine

✦✦✦

Frozen Planet Ice Cream was filled with kitschy decor as Hilary suspected. It was a visual delight actually. Tangerine walls, chrome stools with floral vinyl seats, and a black-and-white tile floor made her mentally drool. If she updated her Pinterest boards more than once a year, she'd have to add a new board inspired by this place. Bubble lights strung near the ceiling encircled the room, and hundreds of stickers were plastered under the glass surface of the counter. A giant fiberglass cone in one corner begged for attention. Hilary took out her phone and spent a few minutes taking photos. She texted some to Jorie, including one of Dane mugging in front of the cone statue, his tongue out and eyes crossed.

Hilary ordered butter pecan in a sugar cone while Dane went all out, getting two scoops—one chocolate fudge, the other bubblegum cotton candy—in a waffle cone with whipped cream and sprinkles.

He took a spoon from the little metal pail on top of the counter.

"I may have been seduced by their selection," he said. "This was bigger than I thought it would be."

Hilary laughed, a little disgusted by his chocolate-cotton candy choice. "I'd offer to help you eat it, but I'm not too sure about that combination."

"What? There's no other way to eat ice cream."

"I'll trust you on that."

Hilary's phone dinged. A text from Jorie.

Who's the hottie next to the cone?

Hilary smiled and tucked the phone in her bag.

They sat at the stools for a while eating in silence until the woman who served them wiped down the counter for the fifth time even though Hilary and Dane were the only ones there. Hilary finally took the hint and suggested they leave.

Outside, clouds had moved in and the wind picked up. A chill crept onto shore too, making Hilary regret the light sweater she'd changed into after the field trip. The fabric was thin, the air seeping through it as she and Dane crossed the street. Ahead, a sign pointed to Gentry Pier.

They walked toward the gate by way of a community garden. A plaque on the gazebo showed it was dedicated to the town by the Broman County Art Guild members.

Hilary stopped to admire the decorative pavers at their feet circling the structure. She'd had the foresight to tie her hair back, thinking about the knots she'd have to untangle in this wind if she hadn't.

Dane opened the metal gate for her. The path ahead of them crossed a rocky causeway for thirty feet until it joined the wooden pier. It was a long, wide pier with sturdy pillars. Gulls perched on a few, watching her and Dane approach. Hilary noted some of the planks were recently replaced, the wood not yet colored with age. Others were weatherworn, small patches of green and orange lichen clinging to the boards.

They walked to the middle of the pier, breaking off bits of their cones to feed to the gulls. The birds swooped around their heads, some of them catching the morsels in midair. Hilary laughed when Dane gasped and ducked. One bird came perilously close to his head, but his reaction was over the top. Tears sprang to her eyes. She sought to steady herself by reaching for the nearest pillar, but she misjudged its proximity and almost toppled over.

Dane's hand was on her arm in an instant.

"I gotcha," he said. His other hand pressed against her back until she was steady on her feet. "Are you okay?"

For a few seconds, warmth infused her arm, then made its way up her shoulder and into her chest. That one-sided smile lighting his eyes in the predusk light was pure magic. Inwardly, she scolded herself. His hand on her arm shouldn't cause such an overblown reaction. Her body was a traitor.

She forced herself to look away, still smiling. "Yes, thank you."

"Did you think for a minute—"

He didn't finish the question. One second his hand was on her arm and the next his foot kicked out from under him. His arms pinwheeled madly as he lost contact with the pier. He tumbled back first, arms flailing, with a splash that soaked the hem of her jeans. His eyes caught hers before he went under, huge with shock.

Hilary froze. With one sharp exhale, air was sucked from her lungs. Her body was brick, unable to move. She gasped, her chest compressing.

I can't breathe.

She fell to her hands and knees, peering over the dock into the water that churned with ripples.

Where is he? Please.

"Someone help!" She could barely get the words out. No one could possibly hear her.

Frantically, she looked toward the parking lot. It was empty. Of course it was. She and Dane waited until dusk when no one was around. The fierce wind had chased everyone away from the lakefront.

All alone.

Waves licked the side of the dock. Gulls cried overhead.

I can't do this. Not again.

The thought crashed through her mind, stilling her panic long enough that she slipped off her shoes and jumped into the frigid water before her brain caught up with the impulse.

Her head swelled with instant pain from the water. Hilary held her breath and dipped below the surface, hoping to catch sight of him.

Nothing.

Her lungs felt like they were a fraction of their size as she came up for air. Her feet had touched the rocky bottom, cutting into her toes, but it was nothing compared to the icy daggers slicing her skin.

Again, she plunged beneath the surface. But she couldn't keep her eyes open long enough to see. *Hurts so bad.*

Hilary resurfaced, looking around frantically. She had to get out. The pier was too high to pull herself up. She'd have to wade to shore, find help before it was too late.

Laboring to turn, Hilary fought the weight of her clothes holding her back. She cried out. Every part of her body hurt. She couldn't breathe.

It's not supposed to happen like this.

Not Dane. Not him too.

She struggled against the force of the water, the cold. It pulled her down and she fought against it. Knives sliced her lungs with each ragged breath.

She stumbled on the uneven lake bottom and fell into the water. Hilary fought to find her footing again when an arm gripped her waist, hauling her up and out of the water.

She caught a glimpse of his face before Dane slung her over his shoulder. His lips were pulled back in a grimace as he plowed through the water, hugging her thighs to his chest.

"Have to warm up," he panted. "No time."

"I c...can't feel my legs."

Wind clawed at the fabric plastered to her skin. The pain was so excruciating she could barely form the words.

"Hang tight," he said, gasping.

Hilary forced herself to breathe. It was even more of a struggle with her chest compressed against his shoulder.

The water splashed around his legs. From over his shoulder, she saw the tops of his boots emerge, then the pebbles crunched under his feet as he hobbled out of the lake.

He set her down gently. "Can you stand okay?"

Her lips couldn't even form the word "yes," so she shook her head instead.

"We need to get back to the Jeep fast. Here," he said, wrapping his arm around her back. "Hang on to me."

Hilary felt like she'd done as he'd asked, but she wasn't sure, her arm paralyzed with cold. They sprinted together toward the car. Dane fumbled with the door handle for a few seconds before he was able to open it. Hilary dove inside.

In the driver's seat, Dane cranked the heat. The air gusted against her wet clothes, making the relief of the warmer car short-lived. She sat there silently, catching her breath, fogging the windows. Her teeth clattered together so hard she thought they would shatter. Hilary leaned her head against the seat while he hunted for something in the backseat. A fleece blanket landed in her lap.

"It's not much but it's something. You'll want to get out of as much of your wet stuff as you can."

She eyed him, shivering. He was right. Her body would never warm up if she stayed in these wet clothes. It was twenty minutes back to Blueberry Point Lodge.

"I'll hold the blanket up. For privacy," he offered.

Hilary glanced out the window. It was still dusk. Their car was the only one in the small lot next to the pier. She supposed someone from the apartments above the shops across the street could see into the car if they really wanted to, but honestly, she didn't care. She was as close to a human popsicle as she ever wanted to be, and that dry blanket called to her.

Dane unfolded it and held it up, his hands almost touching the ceiling of the Jeep and shaking like leaves. She peeled off the sweater. Weighted with cold water, it dripped across her lap before she tossed it to the floor at her feet. Her jeans would stay on. There was no way she was taking them off. Not with Dane two feet away, blanket or not. She probably couldn't maneuver enough to squeeze out of them in the tight confines of the car anyway.

"Okay, I'm good," she said, taking the blanket from him and draping it around her body. "What about you? Don't you need...to do something?" Hilary didn't see another blanket for Dane. He was in danger of getting hypothermia too if he didn't get out of his wet shirt at least.

Dane shifted, trying to wriggle out of it. His fingers tried to undo the buttons, but they were probably still numb. He managed to get a few undone, but the last button flew against the dashboard when he grew frustrated and tore the shirt off. "There's only one blanket," he said. "I'll be good if I aim these two vents toward me."

If she weren't two degrees away from cardiac arrest, a shirtless Dane might cause heart palpitations for a different reason. His shoulders and biceps were roped with muscle, smooth and sturdy. She tore her gaze away lest he think she liked the view a little too much.

They sat there shivering for awhile as heat circulated inside the car. The windows fogged over completely from their breathing. As sensation came back to her hands and feet, the realization of what might have happened hit her full force. She began to shake even more violently as a panic attack gripped her. She bent over, face near her knees, trying to control the ragged breaths wracking her body.

"Hilary?"

His hand was on her back. His strong, steady hand.

"What's wrong?"

Words were impossible. She shook her head, hoping he wouldn't press it.

"It's okay. We're okay." He repeated it, rubbing circles on her back.

The warm air rushed over her, caressing the top of her head. Focus on the sound of the heater, on the feel of his hand. *Control your breaths. Let it pass.*

When she sat back against the seat, he stared at her, worry furrowing his forehead even as he shivered violently.

Hilary flexed her fingers. They were so cold and stuff. She inhaled, concentrating on the scent of his cologne —woodsy.

"Do you want to talk about it?"

Hilary swallowed once, then again as she almost choked on the dryness in her throat. She angled the vent in front of her to blow more directly onto her. "I think we should get back."

He didn't say anything else on the way to the lodge, but Hilary felt him glancing at her every so often. She shut her eyes and images flashed through her mind.

Dimpled smiles.

Lake water as clear as polished crystal.

One red canoe.

A life jacket left hanging on the dock.

A paddle overboard. *Let it go. We'll make do with one.*

But she reached for it anyway—a mistake.

She could still feel the sensation of nothing but water beneath her feet, knowing the lake was hundreds of feet deep. She wasn't the one to forget her life jacket, but panic seized her anyway. She bobbed in the water for a full minute, trying desperately to flip the canoe upright again before realizing she was alone.

A hot tear ran down her cheek as she and Dane sped along Highway 61 toward the inn. The sooner she got back to the busy inn, the sooner the memories might be pushed back into the dark corners of her mind where they belonged.

Chapter Ten

T hey hurried into the house, dripping and
shivering. Darcy met them in the foyer, eyes
wide with shock. It didn't take but a second for
her to realize they hadn't gone for a casual swim, not
with the water temperature in June barely above fifty
degrees.

"What happened?" Darcy asked, walking a half circle
around them before waving her hands in frustration.
"Never mind. You can tell me later. Let's get you
warmed up."

Dane headed for the back door.

"Take care of her first. I'll be in my cabin," he said
over his shoulder as Darcy ushered Hilary upstairs.

Dane trotted across the lawn and headed straight for
the bathroom once inside his cabin. Still shaking, he
cranked up the hot water, clouding the room with steam

as he ditched the last of his cold, sodden clothes. He climbed into the tub, hot water from the shower head raining over him. Twenty minutes later, he turned it off.

He knew what falling into a cold lake could do to a person and how quickly hypothermia could set in. It happened in much warmer temperatures. But Dane hadn't lost his bearings once he went under. He got out quick too. There was a lot of insulation on him; he wasn't exactly lean. Hilary, on the other hand, appeared to be going into shock when he'd surfaced. She stood stiff, mouthing something unintelligible, shaking uncontrollably. It was her reaction that got him moving.

Dane dug into his suitcase for two of his heaviest layers, a long-sleeved polypropylene base layer and a fleece quarter-zip. He pulled on the pair of polypropylene pants, wool socks, and fleece-lined hat, too, that he kept in the side pocket for emergencies. At last he dragged a chair across the room and parked himself in front of the wood stove to light it.

Foremost on his mind was Hilary. He worried about her alone in her room. He'd never witnessed a panic attack before, but Hilary's behavior on the ride back had all the marks of one. Shock was a possibility too, but his immediate concern was hypothermia. He dropped his head in his hands and blew the air from his cheeks. The whole situation could have turned out much worse than it did. A chill ran through him.

A fleeting thought came to him when he tried to

comfort her in the car, and it occurred to him again as he sat there, feeling the welcome heat seep through his layers. Something in her past triggered her reaction. Something she couldn't freely talk about. From what he'd learned so far, Hilary was as cool as they came, but it was a controlled calm.

Dane thawed himself in front of the stove for another half hour. He really wanted to check on her. He wouldn't be able to sleep if he didn't at least see she was comfortable. He slipped on his coat and shoes, and his hand was on the doorknob when someone knocked.

"Hi there," Hilary said when he opened the door. "Can I come in?"

Her hair was still damp under the knit cap. She burrowed her chin and nose into the enormous wool coat that looked like it could swallow her whole. Only her eyes were visible, big blue moons looking back at him. Under normal circumstances he would have been tongue-tied. He'd never seen anyone prettier than Hilary at this moment. He opened the door wide to let her in.

"I was about to head over to see how you're doing." Dane looked her over. "I should have known Darcy would take care of you."

Hilary smiled as she walked into the single room, her gaze sweeping over the interior. There wasn't much to the cabin—a love-seat sofa bed, end table, kitchen table, and two chairs—but it was perfect for the week. The perfume from her hair filled his senses when she took off the hat, her hair tumbling onto her shoulders in soft waves.

"I'm fine," she said. "It's toasty in here."

"I just turned the thermostat up to 'broil.'"

She looked him up and down. "I wondered how you were doing too." Her shoulders settled.

"Do you want to sit?" He motioned to the sofa while he pulled out a chair for himself. Her smile wavered when she looked at him. While she made a noble effort to appear fine, her shaky hand told him she was still unnerved by the whole experience. Hilary tugged the coat closer to her neck and sat on the sofa. He was again reminded of when he'd seen her at the airport, how small and alone she'd looked. But the annoyance was gone. Her irritability about coming to the conference alone seemed to have disappeared a little with each passing day.

She glanced around the cabin. "Sometimes I wish I could live in a place like this," she mused. "A little one-room house with only the barest of necessities."

Dane chuckled. "I think the same thing sometimes. But then I realize I couldn't live without a pool table or my grandfather's shot glass collection."

"You collect shot glasses?" Her grin broadened.

"What? You don't?"

Hilary giggled and looked down at her hands. She paused. "Thank you, Dane. For being the calm one."

"What can I say? Lavender runs through my veins."

"I'm serious."

He leaned forward, resting his forearms on his knees. "I'm sorry. My go-to response for a crisis is to joke."

Hilary nodded. It took awhile for her to speak again. "I feel like I need to explain—"

"You don't need to explain anything. It was a very normal reaction."

She raised her hand to stop him. "Dane, please. Let me talk."

There were footsteps on the porch and then a knock. Darcy came in, her arms laden with fresh towels.

"I didn't know if you needed any," she said, thrusting them into his hands as soon as he opened the door. "Actually, these are an excuse for me to check on you. Are you okay? Hilary said you slipped." She gave him a once-over. "You didn't hurt yourself?"

"Only a bruised ego." He rubbed the back of his neck, his eyes still on Hilary. Where was their conversation headed before Darcy interrupted? As much as he appreciated Darcy's concern, he really wanted to hear what Hilary had to say.

Darcy's shoulders dropped. "Thank goodness. You two are really lucky."

Hilary stood. "I think I'm going to go lie down." She walked around Darcy, heading toward the open door.

Darcy put a hand on her arm. "No, really. Stay. I didn't mean to interrupt."

Hilary hugged herself. "You didn't. I'm suddenly really

tired. Thanks again for this coat. It's really doing the trick."

"You're welcome," Darcy said.

Hilary paused a second longer, holding Dane with her gaze. The moment was suspended and something passed between them. He couldn't name it exactly, but it was like an unspoken understanding of more to come. Her eyes did look weary. They also held answers to the questions running through his mind.

"We'll talk soon," she said to him.

After Hilary closed the door behind her, Darcy turned back to Dane, pressing her hand against her chest.

"She was really shaken up. I'm talking about a full-blown panic attack in her room. Luckily, she took something to help. I was right there."

"I'm pretty sure she had one in the car coming back here too," he said, setting the stack of towels on the table.

Darcy shook her head. "At first, I thought the accident had been much worse, judging by her reaction. Like you lost consciousness or something."

Dane crossed the room to the counter to fill his coffee pot with water. "No, I wasn't even close. I slipped and fell off the pier. Pure clumsiness. She jumped in after me. We were out of the water and into the car pretty quickly."

She gritted her teeth. "There's a reason I've never done a polar plunge benefit. I can't imagine how cold that water was."

"I don't care to do it again, I'll tell you that much." He dumped coffee grounds into the paper filter, slipped the filter into the machine, and hit the button. With caffeine at this hour, he wouldn't sleep tonight. But there was still a chill in his bones, and a hot beverage might do the trick.

Darcy came over and leaned against the counter, crossing her ankles. "After she calmed down and apologized, I finally understood where she was coming from. Poor thing. It's no wonder."

Dane glanced at Darcy. What had he missed?

"What's no wonder? I don't know what you mean."

Darcy looked up sharply. "She didn't tell you?"

"Tell me what?"

"Her husband drowned, Dane. He's been gone two years."

Chapter Eleven

✻

Hilary didn't talk about Will anymore. She avoided the mention of his name even before it came up in conversation, steering away from Will-related topics like college basketball, dogs, and hiking in the North Cascades. She'd gone to grief counseling for the better part of a year and truly felt it helped, but when a marketing-for-small-business class at the community college conflicted with her grief group, she chose marketing. She knew it wasn't healthy, feeling like this, not being able to talk about him. Hilary intended to start up again with the meetings, but then it was harvest time, and she was laid up with bronchitis, and there were other excuses that didn't show up on the calendar but were bigger priorities.

On the other hand, Jorie referenced Will at least a half dozen times each day. It was almost as if her brother was still alive and would walk through the kitchen door on his way in from the barn any minute, joking about why his dinner wasn't on the table, wearing that crooked smile of his. Hilary's heart ached with that mental image so she pushed it away as she'd done so many times before. It didn't seem right to ask her sister-in-law to stop talking about him so much. It was no less normal to talk about him so easily than to not mention him at all. Grief took many shapes, especially in the Larkin household.

Hilary sat in one of the wicker chairs on the brick patio, mesmerized by the early morning sun lighting the tops of the cedars and firs near the shore. She shivered. It was still cold, so she pulled the wool blanket around her. She'd found it draped over the back of the chair when she'd come outside as if it waited for her. She smiled. Darcy seemed to think of everything.

Again, a solid sleep eluded her. She'd tossed in bed last night but managed to stay in her room this time, not wanting to confront anyone—including Dane—in the kitchen while making tea. She was still shaken from the accident yesterday. It was too similar to what she'd gone through already. Her two panic attacks proved that the manner in which she lost Will was still a trigger.

She'd been on the verge of telling him about Will and the accident before Darcy walked in. In hindsight, Hilary was happy for the interruption. Telling Dane at that moment would have been a gut reaction to their bad experience. Another panic attack gripped her upstairs and she'd already overshared with Darcy before she'd gone to Dane's cabin. If she decided to tell him, she wanted to be in a solid frame of mind. Hilary didn't trust herself not to break down again at that point.

But why did she feel compelled to share it with him at all? It weighed on her mind, keeping her up most of the night. Hilary barely knew him. Confiding in people was not something she did lightly. But she trusted Dane even after such a short time. Silly, she knew, but it was the truth. Dane had a quality about him that she'd only come across in a handful of people. He was genuine. She couldn't think of a better word.

When Jorie called late last night, Hilary told her about the events from yesterday. Jorie listened quietly, not interrupting, even when Hilary mentioned how Dane pulled her out of the water and had been so concerned for her, even as he nearly froze himself. She might have gushed about Dane a little too much, judging by how uncharacteristically silent Jorie was about the whole event.

The French doors squeaked open behind her, snapping her back to the present. Hilary knew who it was before she turned to look. Her thoughts must have acted as a homing beacon, drawing him to her. She laughed to herself. Yes, she was definitely losing it.

Dane leaned over her shoulder. "Mind if I join you?" he asked quietly.

"I can hardly say no since I intruded on you the other night."

He sat on the other ottoman, facing her. "Good, because I was going to sit down anyway."

Hilary uncrossed her legs and stretched them out on the ottoman in front of her. She drew an uneven breath, folding her hands into her lap, and gave him a hurried look. He'd put on an olive plaid flannel underneath a dark gray quilted vest. With his hair mussed and light stubble tracing his jawline, he looked like he belonged in an outdoor adventure magazine ad. She pulled her attention away, determined to not get caught staring yet again.

"How long did it take for your clothes to dry out?" he asked. "I think mine will be damp for days, even after spending the night in front of the wood stove."

"Darcy took mine and threw them in the dryer."

"I see. Perks for staying in the inn," he said, nodding slowly. "She sold me on the cabin by touting its privacy. Now I see that we're the forgotten children in the backyard."

She laughed. "I'm sure if you asked her—"

"I'm kidding. I don't have a problem asking Darcy for anything. She's used to my high-maintenance self."

"You hardly seem like that at all."

"Okay, that's a stretch." He paused, cocking his head as he looked at her. "You look like you've recovered," he said, his voice softer.

Hilary nodded. *Recovered* wasn't the word she'd

choose, but she was in a better mindset than last night. "I'm good. Thanks."

He searched her face with an expectant look, like he was waiting for her to elaborate. But she wasn't about to bore him with details of her sleepless night.

"I told Jorie about our adventure. She didn't say much, which was surprising."

"What did you expect her to say?"

Hilary shrugged. "Nothing specific, but Jorie always has something to say."

"Maybe she was glad it turned out okay."

Hilary pursed her lips. "Maybe."

Yesterday had been so busy, and with last night's drama, it hadn't dawned on her until now that the conference was half over. It was funny. Looking back, Sunday seemed like yesterday. But Hilary remembered how she'd felt when she'd arrived at the conference, how the coming week seemed to stretch into an infinite horizon.

"The week is really flying by, isn't it?"

She looked up at him when he didn't respond and caught him staring at her.

"I got the impression you didn't want to be here. But maybe I'm wrong."

She chuckled. "I didn't, but it's grown on me. I was mad that Jorie wasn't here."

Dane's brow arched. "And now you're not?"

"Not really. But it's too bad you won't meet her. She's the dynamo of our team."

"I doubt that's true," he said quietly.

"What?"

"That she's the dynamo and you're not."

Hilary smiled at that. "I'm about as exciting as vanilla pudding."

Dane looked offended. "What's wrong with vanilla pudding?"

She wrinkled her nose. "Bland. Boring. If Jorie didn't talk me into coming here, I'd be back in Idaho, probably cleaning up Hattie's breakfast. And I'd be happy doing it."

"Hattie?"

"My niece. Two years old. Cute as a—"

She paused and wrinkled her nose.

"As a what?'"

"I was going to say button. It's a weird cliche though."

"I agree. An odd analogy."

"Anyway, Jorie has really been my rock. I don't know where I'd be without her."

"I don't think you give yourself enough credit."

She was going to disagree with him because it was her nature to downplay compliments. They embarrassed her, made her feel patronized. But she stopped herself. Dane wouldn't say it if he didn't think it true. Hilary lifted her gaze to him and caught the puzzled frown he wore before he looked toward the beach.

He cleared his throat. "Beautiful day today. Looks like an ideal one for marching around the alpaca farm this afternoon."

"That should make Meg and Yandi unbearably giddy."

Dane laughed. "I'll be on the other bus."

"I think I'll join you."

The silence fell around them again. There was tension between Dane and her this morning, and she didn't understand it. She was overly sensitive about such things sometimes, but the spaces between their conversation seemed loaded with unspoken words. She studied his profile while he continued to look out at the water. His face was the picture of masculine perfection in her mind —thick waves of russet hair, the strong, stubble-covered jaw, a nose almost too small for his face but straight and regal. But what she liked most of all was the reflective expression on his face when he listened. He really listened to her. Hilary missed that in her life. When Will didn't have a million tasks to juggle on the farm, late at night when they were in bed, he and Hilary talked. Will hadn't been the type to discuss feelings. As much as Hilary loved Cal Larkin, Will's father was the stony silent type and it rubbed off on his son. But Will had been an excellent listener for the short time she had his ear. He asked questions. And he liked to problem solve. Hilary desperately missed having him as a sounding board.

Hilary was so lost in her thoughts that she'd been rubbing the finger on her left hand where her wedding ring had been. The sharp pang of loss squeezed her chest when the realization hit her again.

"Hilary?"

She looked up.

"You're shaking your head. Are you okay?"

She let out a short, humorless laugh. Her thoughts had a way of making themselves known lately.

"I lost it yesterday. My wedding ring. It must have slipped off in the water," she said, flexing her fingers.

He didn't say anything right away. Then, "I'm so sorry."

She shrugged with resignation.

"Maybe it's on the beach. Or in the car," he said. "We can check for it later."

Hilary shook her head again. She tried to form the words, but they crouched at the back of her throat.

Dane's lips were pressed together when she glanced up at him. "I'm sorry," he said again.

She felt her lip quivering, so she bit down to stop it.

"You don't need to say anything more—" he started to say as he reached out.

"My husband died two years ago. Drowned while we were on vacation."

Another pause. She heard the intake of his breath.

"Hilary." His hand was on her knee. "No wonder."

The familiar heaviness crept into her chest. There had been a lifetime of tears cried during the first twelve months. She was certain there weren't any left. Hilary shrugged. Now that she'd told him, there wasn't much else to say. Embarrassment ignited her face. What did she expect, telling a near stranger about this deep and personal tragedy?

His hand moved from her leg and gently folded itself around her hand. His thumb rubbed her knuckles.

"Thank you for telling me."

Hilary managed a small smile. His words were comforting. Or was it the warmth of his hand on hers? "Thank you for being here."

She straightened, feeling the tension in her shoulder muscles ease. Hilary pulled her feet from atop the ottoman. "We should get back inside. The program is about to start."

Dane checked his phone as he got to his feet.

His name tag hung crooked on his shirt, the safety pin barely grasping the edge of his pocket. Hilary pointed to it. "You're going to give someone a cramp in their neck if they try to read your badge." Her voice was hoarse. She coughed to clear it.

He looked down and tried to straighten it. "They're so awkward to put on."

Hilary stepped closer, nudging his hand aside, feeling the heaviness of the last few minutes lift. "Here. Let me."

Standing in front of him felt more awkward than she imagined. The pin was tiny, hard to unfasten. She was so close the soft exhalation of his breath moved her bangs. Her fingers seemed to have doubled in size too. It took

LOVE, LIES AND LAVENDER 103

her way longer than she anticipated to fasten the silly thing.

She patted the tag. "There. Good as new."

Dane's hand brushed hers when he straightened his shirt. "Thank you," he said. "Say, maybe we can talk again later?"

His eyes searched hers. Soft concern smoothed over the worried wrinkles on his forehead she'd seen earlier. His expression was so bright and hopeful that her pulse quickened, thudding in her ears. Reluctantly, she tucked her hand in the pocket of her jeans, her skin tingling from the contact.

"Yes, I'd like that," she whispered.

HILARY COULD HARDLY FOCUS ON THE LAST OF the morning speakers, an investment banker from Minneapolis, addressing the group about retirement planning. This was so not her area of interest, but she felt guilted into listening to him. It *should* interest her. At thirty-one years old, most of her earning potential was still ahead of her. Relying on Will's life insurance any longer than she had to was foolish. Still, Jorie got into this stuff, so Hilary scribbled down a page of well-intentioned notes that she'd pass along later to her sister-in-law.

But it was Dane who was foremost on her mind. It was a huge step for her, offering details about what happened to Will to someone who wasn't family or in her grief support group. But he was so easy to talk to.

"He's pretty dreamy," whispered Lucy Riggins, who sat next to her in her usual spot. Lucy sought her out each of the last three mornings. It was too bad she wouldn't see Lucy after this week. They'd really connected. But that was what social media was for.

Hilary's gaze immediately went to Dane, who sat across the room by the large bank of windows. She caught his eye and smiled before she realized Lucy meant the speaker, Trec Kingston. He was indeed striking in a darker, more dangerous-looking Clark Kent sort of way.

"You should talk to him at lunch," Hilary whispered back.

Lucy's eye's bugged out at the notion. "What would I talk to him about?"

"He's a business guy. You want to go into business. Ask him about first steps."

"I already know my first steps. I worked on my business plan over Christmas."

Hilary smiled at Lucy's cluelessness. "That's not the point. It's a question to get the ball rolling." *Listen to me giving relationship advice.*

"I'm really not his type," she said incredulously.

"How do you know?"

Lucy rested her elbow on the table, chin in her hand. "Look at him. He's like a man and a half."

The coffee Hilary sipped almost blew out of her nose.

Hilary dabbed a napkin to her mouth. Across the room, Dane cocked his head, a puzzled smile lighting his face.

The presentation was coming to an end. Papers shuffled around the room as people filled their folders and got ready to transition to the covered tent on the side lawn for lunch.

Hilary pushed away from the table. She put her hand on Lucy's arm. "You're selling yourself short. Give it a try." Weren't those Dane's words to her earlier? *You don't give yourself enough credit.* Oh boy. He was wiggling his way more and more into her subconscious.

Lucy drew a deep, nervous breath. "I'll think about it. I'm going to go upstairs and grab a sweater. See you at lunch?"

"Of course."

Hilary finished gathering her folder and bag. Maybe she should make a quick run upstairs too, freshen up. She made her way between the tables, heading for the stairs, when Dane caught up to her.

"I have an idea," he said.

"The last idea you had landed us in Lake Superior. Why should I trust your idea?"

He grinned wickedly. "Because life is more interesting when you live dangerously."

Hilary lifted her eyebrows, intrigued. "True."

"I'll meet you near the tent in five," he said, rubbing his hands together.

Chapter Twelve

Dane hurried down the hall toward the kitchen. One of the caterers, a no-nonsense worker named Mila, assured him everything would be ready before the last speaker of the morning wrapped up his presentation. Dane hoped he wasn't jumping too fast, but time wasn't on his side.

"Darcy took the basket when she asked me what I was doing," Mila said apologetically when Dane asked if it was ready. "I could hardly say no. I'm surprised you didn't pass her in the hall. She just left."

Dane rolled his eyes. "It's so like her to nose her way into this. Maybe I can catch her before she spoils it. Thanks for your help." He'd discreetly given her a twenty-dollar bill earlier when he asked for her help. Now he'd have to track down Darcy before she revealed his plan.

He came out of the kitchen in time to see her standing

with Hilary, the telltale basket hooked over one arm and a blanket draped over the other. He might strangle his dear friend at the moment if she'd already opened her mouth.

"Your lunch is served," Darcy said, a smile contorting her face into pure glee.

"Excuse me?" Hilary's back was to him, but the confusion in her voice was obvious.

He gritted his teeth. "Nice, Darcy. You totally blew this."

Hilary stepped to the side so she could see them both. "What is this?" she asked, gesturing to the goods.

Darcy looked at the ceiling in exasperation. "I've never been good at keeping surprises. It's my fault for pressing Mila. The blanket is for the beach." She looked at Dane pleadingly. "I'm so sorry."

"And I'm so confused," said Hilary, looking between the two of them.

Dane stared at Darcy until she got the hint. Resigned, she handed over the basket and blanket before she left, dragging her feet like a scolded child.

"I was hoping you'd like to eat lunch down at the beach. It's peaceful there."

Hilary's brows arched.

"I didn't expect Darcy to butt in." He looked down at the blanket and the wicker basket. "Now I feel like my mother is sending me on a date."

Hilary laughed. She tilted her head. "Is that what this is?"

"No. Not really. I mean, I hoped to...again. To talk again." *So articulate, Dane. Well done.*

She nodded slowly as if considering it. "Okay. We can talk. On the beach." She walked toward the doors but stopped to look back at him frozen to the spot. "Are you coming?" Now that they were together again, he was anxious. Maybe this was a mistake, an act of desperation. But he was acutely aware that he might not see Hilary Larkin again after this week ended and it was an impossible thing to imagine. She'd consumed his thoughts since yesterday.

They walked across the lawn in silence. Most of the conference attendees congregated under the tent awaiting lunch. Dane felt conspicuous walking away from the group, obviously heading toward a more private spot. If he weren't so nervous, he might be able to focus on the beauty of the day. Ahead of them, the sun glinted off the water. Artemisia and dusky pink begonias bloomed around the perimeter of the gazebo. A larger garden with iron obelisks and cedar arches beckoned. He'd been wanting to check it out since Sunday. But stopping to look at flowers was furthest from his mind now.

"I really didn't mean for this to seem so orchestrated," he said again.

They'd come to where the lawn stopped and the rocky beach took over. He pointed to a cedar with sparse branches. It shielded the direct sunlight, speckling the ground with shade. It was a warm day, but a breeze chilled the skin exposed above his shirt collar.

"Like a date, you mean." She smiled at him with a hint that she held back a laugh. "I don't think I would mistake it for anything but."

"I was afraid you'd say that." Dane doubled up the blanket and floated it to the ground. "These rocks don't make the softest surface, but it'll have to do."

Hilary sat down and stretched out her legs, crossing her ankles. "It's ten times more comfortable than sitting in those chairs for three hours."

Dane groaned as he eased himself to the ground. He cursed his long legs and the stiffness of his jeans after drying them in front of the fire. Beside him, Hilary snickered.

Despite the discomfort, he laughed too. "If only you were six-three and wearing stiff denim. You'd better believe I'd be laughing at your expense."

"I'm sure it's uncomfortable," she said with a smile. It was good to see her spirits lifted after last night.

They sat in silence for a few minutes, letting the breeze wash over them and watching the herring gulls swoop near them, hoping to share lunch. Dane picked through the contents of their lunch in the gingham-lined basket. He plucked out the bag of gourmet popcorn and tore it open. They took turns tossing pieces, laughing at the birds who grew more gutsy by the minute.

"They remind me of our goats. They don't turn their

noses up at anything." Dane took a handful of popcorn for himself then passed the bag to Hilary.

"They're ornery things, but I still love them." Hilary shook some into her hand. "We used to have some. Jorie and I sold milk soap for a while at festivals and fairs. Then she had Hattie. And I couldn't—" She grew quiet and looked away.

He stopped chewing, studying the back of her head. Of course. If Hattie was two years old, her birth would have coincided with Hilary's husband's death.

"More obnoxious than ornery," he said to keep the conversation going in a positive direction. "Needy, but also very entertaining."

Hilary looked back at him and laughed. "Yes, I remember that."

"So, first goats, now apple orchards and bed-and-breakfasts."

She looked at him pointedly for a few extra seconds. Then she hitched her shoulders. "That's the plan," she said, her gaze returning to the birds who were becoming increasingly more brazen. One bird landed within three feet from her shoes. It cocked its head toward the ground as if suggesting more popcorn needed to be tossed his way.

There it was again. The sense that she wasn't a hundred percent on board with the entrepreneurial idea. He might chalk it up to a lack of confidence, something that could be smoothed out with a solid business plan.

But as he got to know her better, Dane figured there was something else in the way.

"Is the conference helping?" He leaned back on his hands.

"The speakers and field trips have been very inspiring," she said flatly.

A generic answer. It was such a canned response that he smiled. She might as well be reading from a script.

"What's so funny?"

She'd turned back toward him. Saw him smiling like a goon and probably thought he was laughing at her. Now he was embarrassed.

Dane opened his mouth to explain but stopped himself twice. He didn't want to question her motive for being here again.

"You don't believe me." She tossed a piece of popcorn at him, bouncing it off his cheek.

Stunned, he didn't know what shocked him more—the directness of her question or being targeted with popcorn. "What does that mean?"

"Ever since you picked me up at the airport you've been wondering what I'm doing here," she said. Hilary tucked her hair behind her ear, but the breeze carried it across her face anyway. She brushed it back to look at him. "Don't tell me you haven't."

He sat forward. "What have I said that gave you that impression?" He felt like a thief caught with his hand in the jewelry box.

"It's not anything you've said. You're very easy to read."

It would be foolish to deny it. He had wondered no less than a dozen times why she was at a small farms conference when her heart wasn't in it. Here she was handing him the chance to ask her.

Hilary's eyes widened, waiting.

"Okay, fine." He dropped his shoulders. "Let's forget Jorie for a minute. What do you want to do?"

"Work."

"Would I be wrong to say you'd rather do something else besides cultivate apple trees and book rooms?"

Hilary blew the air out of her cheeks. "It's not that simple." She looked away from him and down the deserted beach.

"Let's pretend it is. What's your ideal life?"

She smiled thinly. "I'd love to go back to work in a school. As a social worker." There was no hesitancy in her voice.

"So what's stopping you?"

Her gaze settled in her lap. She sighed again. "I feel like I owe this to…I don't know."

"You owe it to Jorie because it was a shared dream when your husband was alive."

"Exactly. You have no idea how she and Cal helped me after Will died. I literally couldn't get out of bed."

"I'm sure it was horrible for everyone." Dane chose his words carefully. He didn't doubt she felt a strong allegiance to her in-laws. But committing to living someone else's dream if her heart wasn't in it was living a lie. He wasn't going to come out and say that. But he knew she struggled with it. It was written on her face during the seminars. He heard it in her voice when she talked about the farm back home. It wasn't his place to suggest she upend her life, but he heard the resignation in her voice when she spoke of the plans at Larkin Farms. His brothers left the family farm. Their parents didn't guilt them into staying; he certainly wouldn't have wanted them to stay in Clove and work the farm. It would have been a disaster. They wanted to make their life away from Lavender Lane Farm. He applauded them for living on their own terms.

She leaned back on her hands and groaned. "I'm grateful for the life I have there. I don't want you to think I'm not."

He touched her hand. "I know you are."

Hilary looked down. Slowly, she turned her palm upward and clasped his hand, fingers firm against his skin. When she looked at him, her eyes were hooded. Their color stood out against the light of the day, aquamarine pools offset by the dark starbursts at their centers. Dane was hypnotized. He opened his mouth to say...what?

Her gaze dropped to his mouth. Hilary sighed. "I wish Clove and Redville weren't so—"

"—far apart. I know. But they're really not." Her lips

were so close. A strand of her hair tickled his cheek. "Five hours tops."

She drew back, a small smile plumping her cheeks. "You looked?"

He nodded. "I Googled it Sunday night after I brought you back here."

Hilary threw her head back and laughed. It was musical and airy, like the trill of a wren. Dane loved it. What he loved even more was her lips. Colored like the inside of a plum. Moist too. He reached up to trace the minute lines with his finger. If he never saw her again, he'd remember this point in time for the rest of his life. Would she take the hint if he leaned toward her?

"Hate to interrupt this little vignette of solitude and happiness, but—surprise!"

Hilary started. She looked behind them, involuntarily squeezing Dane's hand before dropping it like she'd been scalded.

"Jorie?"

Chapter Thirteen

✦✦✦

Jorie stood behind them, hands tucked into her
pockets. There was no telling how long she'd
been standing there. What had she heard? Hilary
felt herself flush. They'd almost kissed too.

Hilary smoothed her hair. "What are you doing here?"

Jorie took that as an invitation to plunk herself down
on the blanket too. Dane moved away, now with more of
the rocky beach beneath him than the blanket.

"I didn't want to miss all the fun," she said with an
exaggerated amount of cheer. "The updates you've been
sending, the photos from yesterday—I'd been looking
forward to this week for a long time." She shrugged. "I
couldn't stay away."

"But Cal. He was the reason you missed your flight."

"Dad's better. Tom's keeping an eye on him." Her gaze
scanned the blanket, noting the picnic hamper.

"Hattie too?"

"She's with my parents."

That was a relief. But still. The shock clung to her nerves. By the look on Dane's face, he wasn't handling it any better. There was a stiffness to his smile.

The rest of lunch was hurried and awkward. They made polite conversation with Jorie after she was introduced to Dane. Hilary rushed through the meal. She nearly choked on the dense sandwich bread after she'd finished off her bottle of water too soon. Jorie took a few kernels of popcorn when Dane offered the bag to her and waved off the suggestion that she split Hilary's chocolate chip cookie. Hilary tucked the cookie back into the basket. Her appetite was gone.

When it was time to board the bus for the afternoon trip to the farm, she and Jorie were the first ones in line.

"So, tell me everything. I'd like to see your notes later too," Jorie said when they'd settled into their seat. She squinted to look through the window beside Hilary. Outside, Darcy pointed to the other bus now parked behind them. People drifted out of line to board the second one. Dane gave her a wistful smile through the window and followed the other group. "I can't tell you how much I wanted to be here," Jorie said.

Hilary turned away from the window after watching Dane head toward the other bus. "So Cal is doing better?"

"Much. He's back in the thick of things."

That didn't surprise Hilary. Cal worked through his physical ailments more often than not. A hospital stay was the only condition that would keep him inside. He was one of those hardy, grizzled types with weather-beaten skin and a closet full of patched and faded work clothes. *If I ain't dead, I work,* he liked to say often in his loud-as-thunder voice.

She studied Jorie. Five years older than Hilary, Jorie wore her age well despite a life lived in the sun without the sense for sunscreen or hats. Blonde streaks would lighten her tawny hair during the coming months and her lean arms would grow darker with a tan. Jorie helped Tom and Cal around the farm with planting and harvest when she could, toting Hallie to Tom's parents' home in nearby Gifford when the schedule grew especially busy. She loved the physical labor almost as much as balancing the farm's books. Hilary envied her a little for that reason. She wished she took a little more pleasure working around the farm like Jorie did. Maybe she'd feel differently if Will were still alive.

Hilary blinked, clearing her thoughts. "I thought you were so reluctant to pay for another ticket?"

Again, Jorie looked beyond Hilary to the window and made a face. "Missing out was a greater cost. It'll be another write-off. Anyway, you sounded like you needed me on Sunday."

Boy, had she needed Jorie on Sunday. She'd been so full of resentment. Guilt still gnawed at her for feeling that way. Cal had been laid up—in the *hospital,* for goodness' sake—and all Hilary could think of was being stuck living outside her element for a week. In a beautiful inn in the Northwoods, no less. Some punishment. Darcy and Lucy were a dream to meet, and there was Dane, of course. He was definitely the icing on the conference cake.

"Thanks for coming." That was all she could think of to say. Hilary gave her a quick smile then looked outside again.

Dane lumbered forward at the end of the line, his canvas backpack hugging the space between his big shoulders. Yandi and Meg flanked him, pinning him in the middle of one of their conversations. He threw his head back, laughing. Hilary caught herself laughing under her breath too.

"What's so funny?" Jorie asked, leaning into Hilary's shoulder. She tried to look around her and out the window again.

"Oh, nothing."

Jorie gave her that "you're lying" look that was responsible for the three permanent creases across her forehead. But she knew better than to wait for Hilary to elaborate. Hilary was more stubborn than Jorie was persistent.

"So, tell me about this Dane guy," she asked while flipping through her folder. Jorie closed it and squeezed her shoulders up to almost ear level. "You two sure looked cozy with your picnic lunch." Her grin was overdone.

Hilary tried laughing it off, but it stuck in her throat, erupting instead into a sound not unlike a honking goose.

"He runs a really successful operation. I've learned a lot from him so far. And—"

"Like what?"

Hilary was taken aback. It was a generalization. She didn't expect to be put on the spot for specifics, and now couldn't name one single thing she'd learned from Dane. What had he talked about during his keynote on Monday? Gah, her gray matter betrayed her. Think. *Think.*

Jorie waited, eyes wide. Finally, she said, "Well, I'm sure it will help us with our plans whenever you think of it."

"I'm sorry," Hilary said, rubbing her temple. Maybe if she massaged her head, something intelligent would break through her cerebral constipation. She almost laughed out loud at that. "I wasn't expecting you to show. I'm still a little surprised."

Jorie laid a hand on hers. "I know. I should have texted. But when I found out Dad was being released, Tom encouraged me to come. I rented a car, by the way. The Stetmans couldn't pick me up in Duluth, so I had no choice."

"You *are* three days late. That's not their fault."

"I know, I know," she said, her voice clipped. "Anyway, that'll save them the trouble of taking us back on

Saturday." The skin between her eyebrows wrinkled. "I thought you'd be happy I'm here."

"I am happy."

Jorie sat back against the seat, still looking at her. "Okay. You seem—I don't know—distracted."

"I'm fine."

Hilary turned away and spent the next twenty minutes daydreaming. She replayed the picnic lunch scene in her mind, how the two of them huddled close on the beach like a romantic scene on the big screen. Where might the afternoon have led if Jorie didn't show up? Hilary sank against the seat, delighting in the warmth flooding through her as she remembered his hand on hers, his velvet smooth voice in her ear.

The bus turned into a long gravel lane. Ahead, stark white fencing ran across acres of grassy fields and surrounded the tidy red buildings. A small herd of alpacas and two donkeys grazed contentedly in the closest paddock. The wide girth of one of the donkeys could only mean a birth was imminent.

Fred and Elaine Behar were like Mr. and Mrs. Claus in canvas shirts and denim. They delighted in showing off the alpacas, "their kiddos" as they called them. Soon after the tour began, Fred trotted Lottie, a cocoa-colored female, out of the paddock on a lead.

"She's the farm ambassador," he said, saying the rest of the herd appreciated Lottie keeping the limelight away from them. Alpacas are typically shy, Fred said. They stick together when threatened.

Lottie let Hilary run her hand over her soft dense coat. The animal hummed, watching Hilary with its luminous eyes then craned her neck to check on the rest of her friends.

"What about that one?" Yandi asked, pointing to the farthest corner of the corral. A solitary llama stood watchful.

"He's our guard dog. Nothing is going to mess with the alpacas as long as Chester's on duty," Elaine said. She whistled. Chester stood erect, his ears twitching. Slowly, he lumbered toward them. "Be warned though. He's ornery."

Dane, standing against the fence, arm propped along the top rail, turned his full attention to Chester. The animal took his time approaching the fence, not fearful of the dozens of strangers watching him. When Chester was within ten feet, Dane stuck out his hand, tempting the llama to come closer.

Fred Behar snickered. "Like she said, Chester can be something else."

There was no way Hilary would get that close to Chester. She knew the animals had a reputation. Their neighbors back in Redville had a llama. Dickens was an escape artist. Hilary counted on a llama sighting on their property at least every few months. One time Dickens was found in the next county amongst a herd of sheep, snacking in their ryegrass field.

Dane cooed at the animal, waving his hand to entice Chester.

"Such a handsome guy you are." His fingers were inches from Chester's neck.

"He's going on four years old. We got him from a sanctuary in California last year," said Fred.

Chester raised his nose as if smelling the air. Or maybe he was checking out Dane. His crooked yellow teeth gnawed on whatever was in its mouth.

"How do they get along with goats?" Dane asked.

"Fine as far as I know. They're pretty docile animals," said Fred. "But they can be wary of strangers. They show their annoyance by—"

Chester elicited a grumble deep in his chest. He cocked his head back a little more, keeping his eye on Dane. A collective intake of breath rose up from the crowd, including Hilary. She knew what was coming and was about to warn Dane to step back.

Too late.

Chester coughed, spraying Dane with foul-smelling hay and brown mucus.

Dane doubled over, swiping the stuff from his face and coat. Bits of straw clung to his hair. Hilary could smell it from where she stood. She couldn't stop laughing.

"—spitting," finished Fred. He pulled a rag from his back pocket. "Here."

Dane screwed up his face, dry heaving. "It really smells." His voice was muffled as he wiped the vile stuff from his face.

Fred clapped Dane on the back. "Told ya he was ornery."

Jorie leaned into Hilary, chuckling. "I was about to warn him too. Some things you have to learn on your own though, right? We're never getting a llama."

She caught Dane's eye and shook her head. Even coated with llama mucus, Dane winked at them. Beside her, Jorie huffed.

"He's a real charmer, isn't he?" Jorie said out of the corner of her mouth.

Hilary nodded, still smiling. He'd rubbed away the surface goo but it collected in his hair, stiffening into points.

"Almost like he was looking for attention. I mean, how can you not know llamas do that?" she joked as the group followed Fred and Elaine. They headed away from the paddock and toward one of the barns.

"Not everyone is proficient in reading camelid body language," Hilary whispered back.

Jorie rolled her eyes but was silent.

The only white building among the five red outbuildings on the property was now a newly refurbished barn. Elaine used it as an art studio and the farm store. Inside, half the space was devoted to selling handmade sweaters, scarves, mittens, and other wool items. The store also sold stained glass ornaments, handmade cards, and other art pieces on consignment for artists along the North shore, Elaine said. The other half of the building housed Elaine's looms. Giant twenty-pane windows let in an ample amount of light. Elaine hosted classes and retreats throughout the year.

While Jorie struck up a conversation with a woman and her husband about their apple farm near St. Louis, Hilary wandered around the store. She stopped near a wooden bowl filled with wool dryer balls. Little alpaca finger puppets were scattered on the counter around the bowl. She picked out two, fitting them onto her fingers.

"Souvenirs for your niece?"

Hilary turned toward Dane, thrilling at the sound of his voice. "Hattie would love these."

He picked up a dryer ball, inspecting it. "I never would have guessed there were so many marketing opportunities with alpaca wool."

"You don't know much about llamas either, do you?" Hilary wrinkled her nose. "You smell like you went swimming in a manure pile."

He feigned shock. "What, it doesn't trigger romantic feelings?"

Hilary felt her face grow warm. She looked over at Jorie, but her sister-in-law was still deep in conversation. "I can't say that it does," she said matter-of-factly.

Dane set the ball back into the bowl. "I guess I'll have to try something else then."

She pressed a hand to her cheek, feeling the heat. "You sure are accident prone," she said, hoping to change the subject. She didn't like flirting with Dane under Jorie's watchful eye.

He leaned against the table, crossing his arms. The table skidded slightly from his considerable weight. His eyes bulged as he quickly stood upright. Hilary shook her head in disbelief, laughing.

"What can I say? It's a special talent," he said as he pulled the table back to its rightful place.

From across the room, Jorie left the Missouri couple and hurried over to her and Dane.

"I got some great feedback from that couple on apple farm operations. We're going to meet up with them at dinner to talk more." Jorie clutched Hilary's arm to her side, looking at Dane. "You've had her for three whole days. Now it's time for us to catch up on what I've missed so we can move forward."

Dane's gaze darted from hers to Jorie and back again. He flashed a quick grin, throwing up his hands in surrender. "Of course. Don't let me get in the middle."

Jorie pulled Hilary away, rattling on about pruning season and pest control. Hilary glanced over her shoulder at Dane. He stood there, arms crossed, watching them leave the store. His expression was unreadable, but if it was similar to the disappointment she felt inside, he was wondering when they'd get another moment alone now that Jorie was here.

Chapter Fourteen

᠃᠂᠃

Dane pushed back the curtains inside his cabin as soon as a rosy hue seeped through the cracks around the window. The morning dawned bright with an effervescence only seen by those who rise with the sun. He took a deep breath. Off to the right, Blueberry Point Lodge stood on the expansive lawn, its sandstone walls bright with golden light. He scanned the second-floor windows, trying to calculate which window was Hilary's. For a second, he let himself imagine that she stood there in the window, looking back at him as he looked at her. It would be an intoxicating vision, sharing a silent, sensual moment like that. Frustrated, he sighed.

That wasn't going to happen as long as Jorie was here.

Dane moved away from the window and slipped into his boots. He'd take a walk down to the beach before everyone boarded the buses for a farm-to-table breakfast on the outskirts of town. It would give him time to think.

Outside, birds chattered. He filled his lungs with the clear Northwoods air. Dane stepped off the porch of his cabin and walked toward the beach. He found the spot where he and Hilary sat yesterday, talking, and realized he could have stayed on that blanket all afternoon. She was finally opening up to him, but then her sister-in-law ruined the day.

Jorie was a hard read. He didn't miss the looks she gave him during the field trip yesterday. Her sunglasses hid the direct stare, but he knew by the angle of her head that she studied him off and on throughout the afternoon. Then at dinner last night she kept Hilary inaccessible, suggesting she sit here and he there, with someone always between them. Every opportunity he lost to be with Hilary frustrated him.

The rocks ground together underneath his feet. The water was calm today, undulating as it crawled up the shore before it was pulled back into the lake. Dane picked up a thin, gray basalt stone. He threw it into the water, glancing it off the surface one...two...three times. He'd never been good enough to get more than three or four skips. The riverbanks back home didn't yield good skipping stones.

Dane raked both hands through his hair. What was he doing?

He'd barely dated in the last few years, and then all of

the sudden he flips for someone he barely knows. Who has an intrusive sister-in-law. And lives in another state. *Nice work, Dane. You don't make it easy on yourself.*

If they spent another week together, their connection might have strengthened. They were perfect for each other. She'd told him so. Not directly, but in the way she leaned into his shoulder when she talked to him. Or how he caught her staring at him when he looked her way each time during the morning sessions. She'd startle and look elsewhere only to catch his eye two seconds later and smile like she knew it was such a teen crush thing to do. She'd asked him in detail about the lavender farm and they weren't questions from a professional standpoint.

How do you not wake up happy every day in a place surrounded by lavender fields?

Have you ever wanted to do anything besides own a lavender farm?

I bet I know what your wedding flowers will be when you get married someday.

That last one threw him for a loop when she hooked her arm around his as they lingered next to one of the stalls inside the alpaca barn. The rest of the group had already left, heading toward the farm shop again to buy souvenirs before returning to the inn. Jorie was deep in conversation with Meg and Yandi, the three of them silhouetted against the outdoor light as they left through the barn door. Dane sensed the shift in Hilary's mood as soon as she was out from under Jorie's scrutiny. She'd sidled up to him, her hip touching his as they watched the new mother alpaca nuzzle her days-old cria. Dane couldn't even remember how the subject of flowers came up. He didn't bother mentioning that lavender had no part in the wedding arrangements or bouquets when he'd married Felicia.

He walked the beach for another fifteen minutes, then doubled back once he noticed the buses pulling into the driveway near the inn. Dane was first on the bus this time. He grabbed a seat near the front and only moved next to the window when Hilary boarded.

"Do you have room for me?" she asked as she plopped down next to him, her coffee sloshing through the hole in the lid. She grumbled, brushing the spot from her jeans as she dumped her bag at her feet. She wore a sky-blue fleece jacket this morning. Hilary caught him looking at it. "It's Jorie's. She always overpacks."

He smiled and looked through the window. Outside, Jorie's pinched expression was in sharp contrast to those closest to her. The line was slow-moving outside the bus, but everyone looked well rested and in good spirits, most carrying steaming coffee cups too. Jorie was near the back, clearly irritated.

"It's a good color on you."

Hilary stopped midsip to look at him. The jacket only deepened the blue of her eyes.

"Thank you." She looked him up and down. "I didn't see you after dinner last night. Did you turn in early?"

He wasn't about to tell her he thought Jorie was sabotaging his attempts to talk with her. "Sort of. I figured you and Jorie had more catching up to do. I didn't want to get in the way."

She frowned a little. "I'm happy Jorie is finally here for one of these tours. If she wants to get into agritourism, she needs to talk to these people, not just hide behind the financials."

Dane chuckled. "Listen to you."

Hilary's jaw was set in righteous indignation. "I've told her countless times that I don't have a head for the business side of this, except for maybe a little marketing. I'm more of a follower than a leader in this scenario."

"So you like the grunt work, taking orders."

She nodded emphatically. "Just give me a list and I'm good."

Dane leaned toward her. "It sounds like you two are overdue for a conversation." The pressure from her arm against his was a delightful distraction. He wracked his brain to keep up the private conversation so they could stay linked.

"That's on my list when we get home," she said, smiling.

Ahead, Jorie made her way down the bus aisle. She looked pointedly at Dane, then at Hilary sitting next to him. The dissatisfaction on her face wouldn't have been more apparent if the word was written across her forehead with a black Sharpie. She took the empty seat behind them.

"How early can you be up in the morning?" he whispered.

She gave him a sidelong glance, grinning. "As early as need be. Why do you ask?" she whispered back.

"I heard the point near Clearwater Lighthouse is the place to be at sunrise."

"This sounds like a date." Her head was almost touching his.

Dane breathed in the floral scent of her shampoo, almost sighing. "It is if you want it to be."

Her grin widened. She stared at him. "I might," she whispered back.

He concentrated so fully on her pink lips and the pearly teeth behind the bewitching small smile that her words didn't register right away.

Hilary leaned forward to pull a piece of paper from her folder, flipping it over to the blank side. Her pen clicked and she wrote:

Let's keep it on the down-low. I don't think Jorie is ready for this.

He took the pen, letting his fingers linger on hers for a few seconds more than necessary. The sensation was electric. They exchanged a look, and Dane felt the effects all the way down to his heels.

Ready for what, a date? She's not invited. Just saying.

Hilary giggled. Took the pen back.

It wouldn't thrill her to know I'd rather watch a sunrise than have breakfast with her.

Dane hoped Hilary wouldn't be happy watching any old sunrise. He wanted to think it had something to do with him.

She must have read his mind.

There's no one I'd rather watch a sunrise with, by the way. She punctuated the end of the sentence with a little heart. It made *his* heart beat at a full-on gallop.

The bus pulled out of the gravel driveway, and Lake Superior made its grand reappearance above the trees once they were on the highway. Over the speaker, Sean narrated a history of the lake's more famous shipwrecks. With each pothole and curve, Hilary pressed against his side even more. Then the bus pulled into the parking lot at The Fresh Fork and Dane cursed the too short ride.

The Fresh Fork was a destination restaurant with a reputation reaching all the way to the Twin Cities, four hours away. The owners, Lee and Kim Flors-Mattingly, had moved from Austin, Texas, five years ago for a change of pace. Lee had worked in the restaurant scene in Dallas, Scottsdale, and San Francisco before they married and was a trained chef. Dane looked forward to this stop all week. If there was one thing he appreciated, it was a good meal made with the freshest ingredients. A glimpse of the couple's raised beds near the barn was a sign he wouldn't be disappointed.

"I read an article about this place back at the inn,"

whispered Hilary, who'd stuck by his side even after they left the bus. "Their hours are crazy limited. I think I remember it being Thursday through Sunday for dinner only."

"When you've hit a niche market with a unique offering, you can afford to be exclusive. I bet they're taking reservations for Christmas already. The waiting list has to be a mile long."

Hilary shielded her eyes from the sun with one hand, looking up at the log cabin-style structure.

"The article said they also have a few rooms for lodgers. I'm sure Jorie will be all over this if she isn't already."

Dane looked down at her. "And you're not?"

Hilary dropped her hand. "Oh, I am. But Jorie is more into the big picture stuff than I am."

"Just give you a list, right?" Dane joked.

She smiled. "Exactly."

The restaurant was separated from the main house by an open-air breezeway. Potted boxwoods and forest animal sculptures made from recycled metal were set along the stone path and the wooden ramp leading to the restaurant's porch. The Fresh Fork sign, hanging above the entrance, was spelled out in wine corks.

Lee led the group around the gardens, ten evenly spaced raised beds that were in constant use from April to October, he said. They used detachable cold frames during the months when weather was iffy. Lee kept a pretty impressive herb garden too, each herb contained within the tidy circle of an old oil drum cut in thirds. Dane sensed Lee and Kim's reuse-and-recycle philosophy was part of their branding.

Jorie poked her way in between Hilary and him.

"This is exactly what we're going for," she said, her face flushed.

Hilary's eyes bugged. "A *restaurant*? I thought it was a B & B."

"No, no." Jorie glanced back at Dane and rolled her eyes. "The vibe. The look. Everything." Her phone was poised at eye level. She stood rooted to the spot, taking photos in all directions, even as he and Hilary walked ahead.

"We need an herb garden and chickens if we're doing breakfasts. Oh, and I'll need to put in strawberry plants for next season *pronto*."

Beside him, Hilary inhaled and let out a not-so-quiet breath. He glanced at her, but she'd already looked away.

"Classy yet understated," said Jorie under her breath when she caught up to them. "Dane if you don't mind, I'm going to steal Hilary for the rest of the tour. We both need to be taking notes about this."

Dane shared another look with Hilary as Jorie pulled her away. Hilary was so not on board with her sister-in-law's scheme it was sad. Hilary needed to grow a backbone and fast. But she hadn't asked for his advice, so he was going to keep his mouth shut. What he did have a say in though was Jorie's attempts to separate them. Between the annoyed looks and the butting in, it was obvious Jorie didn't want them together. And as patient as he was, Dane was losing it fast.

DANE SPENT AN HOUR AFTER DINNER TALKING with a couple who'd asked him earlier in the week about his goats. George and Lottie Muenchen from Goshen, Indiana, kept a small herd of LaManchas, the breed of goat Dane had on his farm. They wanted to grow the herd to sell milk products, something Dane and his family experimented with when Dane was a teen.

They talked for an hour in the downstairs parlor until the couple thanked him for taking up his time and went to their room. Dane wandered into the kitchen to warm up some coffee before he headed to his cabin. It was still too early for bed, and he'd hoped to see Hilary again, but she'd disappeared after dinner. Most guests had already escaped to their rooms or were walking the grounds in the twilight. Even Darcy and Sean were nowhere in sight.

He pushed open the parlor's French doors to the outside and stopped.

Jorie sat on the short brick wall surrounding the patio, looking out toward the lake. She turned when she heard the door open. Dane wanted to backpedal and find another door and an escape route. But it was too late.

She saw him and smiled. "Dane."

"Hi, Jorie."

If he'd met Jorie Fenwick another time and didn't know she was Hilary's sister-in-law, he might have been attracted to her. She was tall and lean and exuded energy. She was pretty in a no-fuss way, with dark blonde hair that swung past her shoulders when it wasn't swept back in an unpretentious ponytail. But that jealous streak was obvious and unattractive to boot.

"I thought you might already be enjoying peace and quiet in your cabin. They keep their speakers on task here. You're a pretty popular guy."

He didn't plan on sitting, but she patted the spot next to her.

"I'm happy to be of service. Keeping farms sustainable these days isn't easy." Dane crossed his arms and looked at her. "Sorry you missed so much of the week. I hope Hilary has filled you in."

Jorie shrugged nonchalantly. "I'm not too worried. Hil took good notes. The conference was more for her benefit anyway."

"Really?" He thought Darcy planned a good balance of financial and marketing workshops. "Talking with Hilary, I figured you'd be interested in the business sessions."

"Oh? Did Hil tell you about our plan?"

Her gaze lingered on him. It made him uncommonly nervous. She'd been nothing short of nice to him since she arrived yesterday in a forced kind of way. He didn't like how she watched him, especially when he was with Hilary.

Dan crossed his ankles. "A little."

She looked back out at the lake. "I'm sure I would have learned a few things. But Hilary needs the leg up in this venture. I signed us up with her in mind."

He laughed a little. "Is she not on board?"

Jorie's grin faltered. "Oh, I wouldn't say that exactly. Hil needs a little push sometimes. She doesn't have a farm background so, you know, I think she feels a little out of sorts."

"She told me she used to be a school social worker."

"Yes," she said. Jorie brushed her hands together and stood. "For a while."

"Do you think she wants to get back into that?"

Jorie frowned. "She doesn't talk about it. If anything, she's excited about the B & B. It was their dream, after all." She looked at him as if she waited for his reaction. "She told you about Will, right?"

"Yes, she did."

"Oh, good. Anyway, they planned all of it together. When...the accident...well, that's when I stepped in." Her voice drifted away. She paused and cocked her head. "You two have chatted quite a bit."

Dane nodded.

"That surprises me. Hil's not exactly outgoing."

"I've been trying to interact with everyone here.

Sometimes you make a stronger connection with some people more than others."

"Yes," Jorie said, nodding slowly. Her eyes bore into him and her smile grew stiff once again.

The silence stretched. In the distance, a screech cut through the stillness. An owl perhaps. Dane peered into the darkness near the wooded portion of the property. It was cooling off and he hadn't brought his jacket with him to dinner.

"I think I'm going to head inside," she said, standing.

"Same here. Have a good night."

Dane stood at the edge of the patio until he heard the French doors click shut. He watched her through the curtains as she stopped at the tea cart for a mug. She filled the mug with water from the carafe. And then she glanced toward the French doors, and the darkness outside kept her from seeing that he still stood there, looking back at her. Even from the distance, Dane saw the deep furrow of her brow and the downturned corners of her mouth.

Her expression wasn't a coincidence. It was meant for him.

Chapter Fifteen

Hilary stood in front of the bathroom mirror, pulling the comb through her hair. She woke before her alarm sounded and kept the lights off until she was in the bathroom with the door closed. Jorie snored softly on her side of the king-sized bed. Hilary was careful not to wake her.

She'd dressed in the nicest pullover she'd packed, a berry quarter-zip with another Larkin Farms logo on the chest. It wasn't the first time in the last few days she wished she'd packed something more dressy. On the other hand, it was cold on these Minnesota mornings and she brought practical clothes, not anything for sunrise dates at the beach.

Hilary smiled.

A date. She was definitely going on a date with Dane.

She opened the bathroom door a crack and put her ear

against the space. Jorie's even breaths assured her that she might make it outside their room without notice. With a little luck, she and Dane would be back within the hour while Jorie was still in the bathroom, getting ready for the day, none the wiser. She'd tell Jorie she couldn't sleep. She'd gotten up early if Jorie asked.

But this wasn't like her. Lying, especially to Jorie. If it weren't the last day, if she wasn't desperate to see Dane before they said goodbye tomorrow, Hilary would speak up. She'd ask Jorie why every time Dane came near her, Jorie had an excuse to keep Hilary away. Why she wore that frozen smile whenever Dane talked to her. She'd save the questions for the trip home. Now she wanted to see Dane.

He was waiting for her in the foyer. Darcy, still in pajamas and slippers, handed him the keys to the Jeep as Hilary came downstairs.

"Have fun, you two," Darcy said, grinning. Darcy's eyes darted between her and Dane as if Dane confided something delicious to her even as she stifled a yawn. "Debi's Donuts is the spot in town for glazed rings and a coffee if you can't wait until breakfast."

"Duly noted. Thanks," said Dane. He tossed the keys in the air then caught them. He turned Hilary's way, looking over her slowly which sent a warm tingle down the back of her neck.

"Ready?" he asked.

They chatted nonstop on their way to the lighthouse,

talking over one another. It was like being a teenager again and her first time in a car without a learner's permit and a parent in the passenger seat. Dane was so engrossed in their conversation he almost missed the turn into the gravel drive. Hilary whacked his arm and pointed. The tires might have squealed a bit, which made them giggle. Ahead, the lighthouse stood regal and white, a stark contrast against the cobalt backdrop of the lake. They parked in the small lot under a leaning cedar and away from the other two cars. No one was in sight.

Dane pulled a blanket out of the backseat. He waited for Hilary to get out before they started down the path.

"Darcy said we have to walk a little way. There are benches on the other side of the lighthouse near the overlook," he said. Dane pointed to the top of the structure. "See the lantern room? Darcy said they have star festivals here in the fall, and if you're up there on a clear night, you can see the lighthouse on Isle Royale thirty miles away."

Hilary shielded her eyes from the sun's glare to look at the top of the lighthouse. "You two are really good friends, aren't you?"

"We found out real quick the single biggest thing we had in common when we met in navy boot camp was clumsiness." Dane pushed up his coat sleeve to reveal a five-inch-long scar on his forearm. "Crashed right into a plate-glass window when I slipped on a wet floor. Darcy has a scar on her knee after falling on the broken glass on the same wet floor."

"Yikes." Hilary veered away, teasing him. "I hope it's not contagious."

He pulled the sleeve down. "Anyway, she's been a great friend, through the highs and the lows."

"Lows such as stitches?" she joked.

Dane scuffed his feet along the gravel as they walked. "That and...other things."

The lightheartedness left his tone. Hilary glanced at him but he concentrated on the path in front of them.

They rounded the lighthouse, following the walkway past pruned boxwoods and clumps of zinnias and artemisia. A chilly breeze caught Hilary off guard when they were no longer shielded by the building. She hunched into her coat.

"You'll be warm in a minute. Promise," Dane said.

Clearwater Lighthouse sat on a high rocky bluff overlooking the lake. It was a sheer drop from the top of the bluff to the water below. Guardrails stopped visitors from venturing too far near the edge. Dane led Hilary down a few stone steps to a sunken patio. More boxwood bushes surrounded the patio, offering protection from the wind. There were cedar benches arranged in a half circle and a telescope stood near the rail. They had the patio to themselves. The view was stunning.

"Let's sit here," Dane said, unfolding the down blanket.

Hilary settled onto the bench. Dane sat beside her, floating the blanket behind them. Cocooned inside, Hilary instantly warmed, though she suspected it had more to do with Dane beside her than the blanket.

"How's that?" His voice was an intoxicating whisper. Dane clutched the blanket together near their chins and encircled her back with his other arm.

"Perfect." Hilary breathed in his cologne, delighting in the fresh, woodsy scent. To their left, the sky was awash in pinks, golds and lavenders of an early summer dawn. "This is beautiful. I'm surprised more people don't come here to watch."

"I like having the spot to ourselves."

They sat in silence for a few minutes, listening to the waves lap the rocks below. It was easy to get lost in the melodies of nature here. Hilary thought about what might be an equivalent sound back home, something meditative. The fall leaves crunching underfoot perhaps. She never ventured down by the Roan River that ran adjacent to their land, but the rushing water from spring rains might give her the same sense of peace, though the river wasn't more than a trickle as summer wore on.

"What are you thinking about?" Dane asked.

"Back home."

"Home is the furthest thing from my mind right now." He gave her shoulder a gentle squeeze.

"I was just making comparisons between the two places."

"And?"

"I don't feel the same sense of peace in Redville that I do here." Hilary leaned closer to him and felt the rough stubble of his beard against her forehead.

Dane turned into her so his lips brushed her hair. "Maybe you need a change."

Hilary lifted her gaze to him. His lips were so close, his breath caressed her face. Stars erupted in her peripheral vision and she realized she was holding her breath.

"Are you okay?" he asked when she took a deep breath.

"More than okay."

His finger found the underside of her chin. Hilary tilted her head.

"Is this okay?" he asked.

She didn't bother to answer. Some things are better shown than spoken.

Dane closed the small space between them as he leaned toward her.

The kiss was soft at first. Their lips meshed so perfectly together that all sensation flowed to this small spot where their bodies joined. It was a featherlight touch, soft, searching, unyielding. It seemed to suck the breath from her little by little. *When had a natural function like breathing become such a chore?*

Dane wove his fingers through the hair at the back of her neck as the kiss turned more urgent. Hilary's world spun away like a planet let loose from orbit. She wrapped her arm around his back, anchoring herself to his chest. *Oh, his lips were amazing. This can't stop.* But as soon as that thought crept into her mind, she felt him pulling away —*no!*—and his hand untangled itself from her hair, caressing her neck, her arm, until his fingers folded around her hand resting on the bench. His eyes were still closed, but he brought her hand up to his mouth and kissed her knuckles. When he opened his eyes finally, a lazy smile spread across his face.

"That's exactly the kind of change I was thinking about," she whispered.

"Me too."

A soft laugh escaped her. "I don't want to go back yet."

He grew still. Hilary thought he hadn't heard her. Then, "To the inn or home?"

"Both."

"I don't either," he said. "But maybe you'll come to Clove sometime?"

"I'd like that." Maybe tomorrow wasn't the end like she dreaded. It was even more of a possibility now that he'd spoken her thoughts aloud. "And if you visit Redville, you can be an honorary guest at the inn and be the first to review it."

He smiled when she looked up at him but it was a sad smile.

"I'm serious," he said quietly. "I don't want to leave

here and not see you again. Tell me that's not going to happen."

"It's not. I've been stressing about the same thing." She drew back to look him square in the eye. "Why would you think I don't want to see you again?"

Now he looked hurt but he didn't elaborate. Hilary knew he was holding back by the uncertainty she read in his eyes.

"I don't," he said.

Hilary let out a soft laugh. "I never expected this. I didn't even want to come." She slumped. "What am I going to do?"

"About what?"

She'd said too much. Hilary didn't want to subject Dane to that conversation again. Jorie had been pleasantly absent from the conversation so far.

"Never mind." She smiled up at him then snuggled farther into his side. He pulled her close once again. Reveling in the strength of his arm around her and the warm breath against her hair, she sighed. "Let's just enjoy the morning."

HILARY CLIMBED THE STAIRS TO HER ROOM, TWO coffee mugs in hand, one for her and one for Jorie. She half expected to see Jorie downstairs already eating in the dining room, but when she asked Darcy if she'd seen her sister-in-law yet, Darcy said she hadn't.

She'd planned to be back within the hour, but Hilary couldn't bring herself to suggest they leave. The morning had been perfect—the weather, the scenery, *that kiss*. She almost suggested to Dane they ditch the last day of the conference. Maybe get lunch somewhere in one of the little towns along the highway, hike in the state park near the Canadian border. And talk. Hilary missed talking to someone who really knew how to listen. She didn't realize she had so much to say until Dane started asking questions. What were her parents like? Did she always want to be a social worker? Where did she meet Will? How had she dealt with her grief? She couldn't help but think Dane came into her life at the exact time she needed him, at a time when her future depended on her ability to recognize her needs and find the courage to take the fork in the road. The right fork and not necessarily the easiest one.

She balanced the two mugs in one hand and eased the door open. Inside the room, Jorie sat in the overstuffed floral armchair, feet on the matching ottoman, reading.

"Good morning. I brought you coffee." Hilary set a mug on the side table next to Jorie. "Did you sleep well?"

Jorie set the book in her lap. "Well enough." Her gaze rested on Hilary. "Where have you been?"

"Oh, you know, I went for a little walk. Grabbed some coffee. I guess I'm a little restless from sitting so much during the week." She couldn't help but squirm under Jorie's scrutiny. Telling a little lie didn't help matters.

"Hmm. Did you take a walk with Dane?"

"Sort of...yes. Yes, I did."

Jorie uncrossed her ankles, closed the book, and got up out of the chair. "You two have really grown close this week." She went over to the dresser.

Hilary felt her face flush. Disappointment crowded out the guilt though. Why should she feel shame for spending time with Dane?

"He's a nice guy." She shrugged. It could be as simple as that as far as Jorie was concerned. Hilary didn't need to explain herself.

Jorie took a piece of paper from the dresser top and dangled it between her two fingers.

"What is this, Hil?"

Hilary went closer, cocking her head so she could see it. With dawning dread, Hilary realized it was the notes she and Dane exchanged while they sat next to each other on the bus yesterday. She'd said things about Jorie. They'd laughed about it. Horror swelled in her.

"Jorie, those...are my notes."

"Notes? This isn't what it looks like." Jorie scanned the paper. "'I don't think Jorie is ready for this.' Ready for what exactly?"

"It was silly talk. It's not a big deal."

Jorie read over more of their flirty exchange, her eyebrows arching. "'I'd rather watch the sun rise than have breakfast with her.'" She looked again at Hilary. Jorie's pain was palpable.

Hilary sank to the bed, covering her face with both hands. This was beyond bad. The last thing Hilary wanted to do was hurt Jorie. Jorie did so much for her, picking her up when Hilary fell down the dark well of despair. She shuttled her to therapy sessions and grief group meetings. Jorie shouldered the burden of Hilary's work around the farm as well as her own that first year, all the while caring for newborn Hattie. She did it without complaining or making Hilary feel beholden to her. And then once Hilary's mind started to clear, Jorie made the suggestion to move ahead with the B & B plans. It buoyed Hilary, made her feel needed again, filled with purpose.

Jorie's stony silence was worse than anything she could say. Hilary looked up, fighting to see Jorie through blurry eyes. "I'm sorry."

Jorie set the paper back on the dresser and crossed the room to sit down again. She cupped the mug in her hands, watching her over the rim. "So what does this mean?"

Hilary sat upright. "It doesn't mean anything. It doesn't *change* anything."

"You like him."

"Well, yes." That was obvious from the notes they'd exchanged.

Jorie looked down at the carpet, slowly shaking her head.

Hilary waited. "What?"

More silence.

"Jorie, say something. Please."

Her sister-in-law looked toward the window. She waved her hand dismissively. "I think you've forgotten why we're here," she said with resignation in her tone.

Hilary huffed. "No, I haven't."

"I thought we were in this together."

"Of course we are." Her voice rose an octave. She cleared her throat. *Stay calm.* "I'm sorry for the note. Those words weren't...kind."

Jorie's lips pressed together. Then, "No, they weren't, but that's not the issue. This is what Will wanted. I thought this is what you wanted."

Her words were hushed but they were as clear as if Jorie shouted them. Hilary's breath caught.

"Don't use his name like that."

Jorie frowned. "Like what?"

"As a weapon to hurt me."

It wasn't the first time Jorie used the memory of Will to get a reaction. The first time happened last fall when Hilary was set to leave for a long weekend in Tempe to visit her parents. She'd forgotten her promise to watch Hattie while Jorie met with a contractor about working on the newly purchased property. Jorie went through the roof, accusing Hilary of not taking the project seriously. Hilary apologized profusely, Jorie canceled the contractor meeting, and they'd had a heart-to-heart when Hilary returned from her trip.

Since then Hilary committed to being more involved in the decision-making.

She spent hours with Jorie hashing out the details of rehabbing the old Robillaud place. The stately Victorian farmhouse down the road had fallen into disrepair and had been off and on the market for years. The property caught Will's eye when he and Hilary were first married since its land abutted Larkin Farms, but they weren't in a position financially to make an offer. After Will's accident, Jorie made it her mission to buy the place. *Will would want this,* Jorie reasoned. In her fog of grief, Hilary agreed.

All the planning paid off. The bank approved their loan without reservations. In her initial walk-through with Jorie, the condition of the house horrified Hilary. She remembered shrugging off Will's comments about the house after he'd gotten a peek inside one day when the then current owners had been on the property. "It has good bones, Hil," he'd said. "It needs new mechanicals and a little paint." Good bones indeed! Hilary almost laughed out loud when those words popped into her head. She could still imagine the pitch in his voice growing higher as it did when he'd try convincing her of something. She'd blissfully avoided becoming involved in the idea, letting Will and Jorie dream about bumping out walls, chimney repairs, and adding bathrooms. It was all talk; they didn't even own the house. If it ever became a reality, she'd step in when it was time to decorate, thank you very much. Now she felt guilty for her skepticism.

Will had always been the glass half-full type and was excited about the revenue stream a B & B would offer. Redville had one Super 8 near the interstate. The nearest B & B was thirty minutes away in Claremont. When she looked at the dilapidated house, all she saw was a one-hundred-fifty-year-old money pit. But unlike Hilary, Jorie inherited her brother's enthusiasm for fixing the old place.

Jorie huffed, bringing Hilary back to the present. Jorie's expression still looked pinched.

"I would never use Will's name like that, Hil. I'm shocked you think I'd do that."

Hilary hugged her arms against her chest. The shame squeezed her insides, stifling her ability to take a calming breath.

"I'm sorry," she said again. She was always apologizing.

Jorie stood. "I'm getting hungry. Did you eat?"

Hilary shook her head slightly. Were they finished talking? What was resolved? "No, I'm not." She was a little nauseous to be honest.

"I'm not sure you know what you're doing, Hil." Jorie's voice softened again. "We leave tomorrow. Then what? Are you going to be running to—where—Washington to see him all the time?"

"He lives in Oregon." Hilary picked up her bag. "And I haven't thought that far ahead." That was another lie. She could think of nothing but Dane. Earlier this morning she'd mapped out the route she'd take if she went to visit him. Hilary planned to ease Jorie into the possibility she and Dane might spend time together beyond the conference. But after this, it might be impossible without hard feelings.

"Let's make the most of our last day, okay?" Jorie's voice was still strained, the hurt Hilary inflicted still apparent in the clipped measure of her words. "We can talk more about this later."

Hilary pulled her bag onto her shoulder again and followed Jorie out of the room and downstairs. The dining area was busy with guests and the clatter of dishes being cleared by the catering staff. She scanned the tables, praying Dane wasn't here. She couldn't bear to see him after this. Jorie had read their notes. The humiliation still burned her cheeks. If having Jorie and Dane together was awkward before, it would be even worse now.

Her jaw ached from clenching her teeth. What an idiot she was for keeping those notes. It had been an amazing morning at the lighthouse too. She touched her bottom lip, trying to recreate the softness of his kiss. She tried to imagine what might have happened if their time hadn't been limited. And now she was trying to avoid him.

Hilary wondered if she were more angry at Jorie for making her feel guilty or at herself for allowing it.

Chapter Sixteen

The white tent on the lawn glowed against the darkened sky. People were already seated at the round tables and eating. More people drifted across the lawn toward the gathering, stopping to admire the pink-tinged horizon or prolong their hushed conversations before they joined the festive atmosphere under the tent. Dane wasn't ready to eat yet. His stomach was knotted. Instead, he rested an elbow on the bar, swirling the ice cubes in his almost empty drink, watching.

Beyond the tent, waves on the lake flashed like fireflies before they melded into the shore. The steely strains of a banjo from the bluegrass band drowned out the sound of the water. Dane scanned the congregation of people under the tent again. It was impossible that he'd missed her crossing the lawn. He'd come early to grab every minute possible with Hilary. Despite spending almost two hours together that morning, he was greedy for more time. He kept replaying their kiss in his mind's eye, the way her eyes grew hooded and her lips parted when she realized it was inevitable. The softness of her mouth on his. The way she clutched his bicep, pulling him closer, wanting the kiss to deepen. The images swam into his subconscious, infecting his ability to think of anything else.

Dane blew the air out of his cheeks. Where was she?

After they returned to the inn, Hilary disappeared. He'd waited for her to come downstairs before the day's sessions began, but somehow he'd missed her. His texts went unanswered too. The sessions he attended weren't ones she and Jorie chose. They'd spent the day away from Blueberry Point Lodge at an overflow space inside one of the churches in town, learning about catering for small venues like bed-and-breakfasts.

Dane downed the rest of his drink and set the empty glass on the bar as Hilary appeared on the patio, Jorie at her side. He cursed to himself. His work was cut out for him if he wanted privacy tonight. Like a protective parent, Jorie hovered.

Hilary gave him a little wave. Her gauzy floral skirt swished around her legs as she walked toward him. He sighed. Beside her, Jorie narrowed her eyes. Wonderful.

The dissatisfaction on Jorie's face was almost comical. At least he didn't take offense easily or her demeanor might sting. He waited for them to choose a table before leaving the bar to wander over. Hilary had an open spot on either side of her. He grabbed a seat next to her, silently congratulating himself before Jorie could somehow sabotage his chance.

"Busy day," he said to her.

Hilary sat stiffly, her hands in her lap. She smiled though, her gaze sweeping over him as if the sight of him quenched her thirst. Her shoulders relaxed.

"A very busy day. I'm exhausted." She feigned a pout. "I still have to pack too."

Dane didn't want to think about it. Sean was driving Dane and others to the airport at four in the morning. Hilary would head to Duluth later in the morning. He'd be in the air by the time she left Hendricks.

He brushed her hand with his and he saw her stiffen again. She met his eyes and gave him a small, discreet shake of her head.

No.

"What's wrong?" he whispered.

"Nothing," she whispered back, but her eyes widened in an unspoken message. Behind her, Jorie rested her chin in one hand, watching the band.

"Did something happen?"

Hilary squeezed his hand momentarily under the table while looking the other way. *Not now,* he guessed the gesture meant.

Yes, Hilary and Jorie had had words. Hilary had no

problem being near him before tonight. Now with Jorie on the other side of her, Hilary could barely look at him. Whatever it was, Dane wasn't going to learn anything while Jorie clung to Hilary.

When the band took a short break, Jorie rose.

"I'm going to get a drink. Want anything?" she asked Hilary.

Hilary lifted her water bottle. "I'm good."

Jorie glanced at Dane's half-empty glass. "You?"

"Thanks, but no." All he wanted was for her to leave.

Dane waited until Jorie was a safe distance away. Then Dane leaned in.

"Talk to me."

Hilary let out a shaky sigh as if she'd been holding it in since she sat. "She's upset that I've lost focus during the week. I haven't taken full advantage of the conference, she told me this morning." She chewed on her lip like she was fighting back tears.

He felt himself frown as he studied Jorie's retreating back. "She doesn't have any right to say that. She missed almost four full days."

He didn't know the full breadth of their family dynamics, but from what he'd seen and heard in the last six days, Hilary and Jorie didn't share an equal partnership. For whatever reason, Jorie held all the cards and Hilary deferred to her. Dane laid his arm across the back of her chair.

"Hilary, look at me."

She sighed. Her face was drawn.

He rested his hand on her shoulder. "You've done nothing wrong. You have nothing to feel guilty about."

Hilary sat forward, breaking contact with his arm around her. "But she's right. I didn't take advantage of the conference. It's clear to me now."

"Yeah, after she shamed you."

Frustration boiled inside him. He struggled to keep the bitterness from his tone. Hilary took her sister-in-law's approval to heart. Jorie took advantage of it too. It couldn't be any more obvious. And this wasn't what he wished their last night together would be like.

"No. It's true. I didn't want to come," Hilary said. "I resented her for staying behind. And it wasn't her fault Cal ended up in the hospital last weekend. She stayed behind to be with her dad. What kind of person does that make me?"

"You were frustrated because Jorie is your support system. You counted on her being here. What you felt was natural, Hilary. Don't beat yourself up over it."

Hilary dipped her head, looking across the room through her lashes. "She's coming back. We can't talk about this anymore."

"Please tell me we aren't going to tiptoe around her all night."

Hilary bit her lip. Dane didn't like the look on her face.

"I'm getting in line. We can talk more when she's not nearby," he said, rising. "Which is almost never."

Hilary stared up at him with a blank look.

"I'm sorry. I shouldn't have said that."

After a few seconds, she pushed her chair back and got up, striding past him on her way to the buffet line. If Jorie hadn't sidestepped out of the way, Hilary would have knocked her off her feet. Dane followed close behind.

But Hilary wasn't getting in line for dinner. She marched out from under the tent, across the lawn, and into the side door of the inn. Dane was tempted to follow her, but he stopped himself. She needed time to herself. He didn't trust his restraint anyway. As patient as he was, it was wearing thin, and he didn't want Hilary to think his frustration was directed at her. Whatever made her angry, he'd get to the bottom of it before the night's end. They'd say goodbye on good terms. He wouldn't settle for anything different.

Fifteen minutes later, Hilary still hadn't reappeared. He'd struck up conversations with two people, waiting for her to rejoin him at the buffet. When that didn't happen, Dane halfheartedly filled his plate and headed back to the table. Jorie sat there alone, picking at the barbecue on her plate. She barely looked up when he sat down.

"Where'd Hil go?" she asked, moving the food around.

"My guess is to her room. She didn't tell me."

Jorie rolled her eyes lazily. "It's not like her to go stalking off."

Was he being blamed? He waited for Jorie to say something else, but she was too focused on the food she wasn't eating. If she was baiting him, he wasn't going to bite.

"Did she mention that she's mad at me?"

He paused. What business was it of hers what he and Hilary discussed? "No, she didn't."

Jorie pursed her lips. She didn't believe him. Not that he cared.

"I'm not sure you know all there is to know about Hil. She's not very open about...certain things." Jorie set her fork down and leaned back in the chair. "Maybe she mentioned Will's accident though. It was a horrible time for her. For all of us."

"She mentioned it, yeah. I didn't ask for details. She didn't seem to want to talk about it."

Jorie crossed her arms. "That's not surprising. I try to draw her out sometimes. To talk about it, especially when she gets quiet. Hilary was in a very dark place for a long time, understandably. She's always dealt with things internally."

He nodded.

"She's finally coming back though," Jorie said.

Dane nodded again, folding his hands together on the table. Between the person he'd met last Sunday at the airport and the woman who'd spent the morning with him, well, there was no comparison between Hilary then and now. Maybe being away from Jorie drew her out. Granted, he'd only met Hilary's sister-in-law two days ago, but Jorie's domineering nature had to overwhelm someone like Hilary, especially at a vulnerable time in her life.

"That's why I think getting back to the farm with this new business mindset will be good for her," Jorie continued. "I'm surprised at how engaged she seems now."

Funny, hadn't Hilary told him Jorie blamed her for not taking advantage of the conference? That Hilary seemed distracted?

"I have no way of knowing how she was before, so I'll have to trust you on that."

Jorie's expression shifted. It wasn't exactly displeasure, but Dane noticed the smile drop from her eyes.

"She seems to act differently when *you're* around. You two got off on the right foot, I'd say," Jorie said. Her voice took on an extra chipper note, but there was still an iciness to the statement.

What could he say? That night in the kitchen changed things. Whatever walls she'd put up had been breached. He got to know the woman with the kind heart, sense of humor, and a passion for something she believed in. He also thought she'd found the courage to stand up to Jorie, to tell her that Jorie's dream wasn't necessarily her dream anymore. He regretted that he wouldn't be around for THAT conversation.

"Like I said before, Hilary is a lot of fun. Bright, funny." He stifled a smile. "And she likes Northwoods sunrises almost as much as I do."

Jorie's head snapped up. "What?"

A chuckle escaped him. "Oh, nothing. Private joke."

She picked at a nail and was quiet for a few moments. "Listen, Dane. I'm not going to mince words. She's still very fragile. So if something"—Jorie bobbled her head slightly while she looked upward as if trying to find the right word—"started between you two, it's probably a good idea for a clean break."

Dane bristled. Who was she to direct his love life? Poor Hilary lived under this woman's thumb whether or not she realized it.

"Hilary is a grown woman. I think you should leave it up to her if she wants a 'clean break' as you say. I certainly don't."

"Fair enough." She gave him another humorless smile.

Standing, she gathered her plate and cup. "Anyway, I'm happy to have had this little chat. Hilary mentioned you helped a lot with marketing ideas," she said. "Not my strong suit. I can balance the books, but the whole social media thing? Not me at all."

She waved her hand in the air like a limp flag, a

parting, carefree gesture like they hadn't just talked about late husbands and calling it quits on Hilary, the first woman he dared open his heart to since someone shattered it.

Dane leaned back, crossing his arms. "I told her to put my number on speed dial. She can call me anytime with questions."

"Speed dial," she mused as she pushed in her chair. "How nice."

HILARY SPENT A HALF HOUR SPRAWLED ACROSS her bed, sobbing into her pillow for twenty minutes and ten getting her game face on again. She didn't want Jorie to find her in the midst of a crying fit, so she combed her hair, picked the mascara clumps from her eyelashes, and slipped into her shoes again. She spent a minute in front of the mirror smiling at her reflection, but all the practice in the world wouldn't take the sadness from the lines around her eyes.

She hated leaving Dane like she did moments after she and Jorie came down for dinner. Of course he knew something was wrong right away. These days she had trouble keeping her emotions in check. They seemed to flood her thoughts and spill out in the form of tears, sharp words, or laughter that lasted a little too long. Maybe she was going crazy. So far she'd saved the outbursts for Jorie. But she was on the verge of crying when she recounted her fight with her sister-in-law to Dane. And his comment about Jorie always being nearby pushed her over the brink. That it was the last night with Dane didn't help either. *Boohooing* in the middle of the conference wrap-up event would have been bad form. So she left.

She waited until the rosy bands across the sky faded and darkness fell across the lawn of Blueberry Point Lodge to come outside again. Lucy came over to talk with her and give her a hug, wishing her luck with the inn before Lucy left to join the dance party. Yandi and Meg wandered over to say goodbye, too, before they went upstairs.

"Our bus leaves at four in the morning for the airport. Mom isn't an early bird," Meg said, hooking her thumb at her mother behind her. "Come visit our alpacas sometime."

From her spot on the patio, Hilary watched the congregation under the tent. The catering staff cleared the tables of empty bottles and discarded napkins and moved the tables to the perimeter of the tent. Now with room for dancing, the band kicked up their tempo. That prompted some of the restless guests to drag partners into the center of the makeshift dance floor right away. The overhead string lights cast an inviting glow on the surroundings, something Hilary couldn't deny even though she wasn't feeling very festive. She walked toward the tent for the second time that night.

Dane spotted her right away and left his stool at the bar.

He was so good-looking it nearly took her breath away. His moppish head of hair was combed into some semblance of control. That smoky look she loved about him was enhanced by the low lighting of the tent. All day she'd dreamed of kissing him again. Then as the hours progressed and Jorie's stony silence carried into the afternoon, Hilary's mood tanked. Guilt over betraying Jorie overshadowed her daydreams about Dane.

Dane reached for her hand as she came near.

"You've given 'making an appearance' new meaning. That's two times tonight you've caught the attention of every guy under the tent."

She smiled up at him. "Yours included?"

The look he gave her sent shivers across the back of her neck. Silly question.

"Where did you go?"

"I had to… I needed a break." She wouldn't lie.

"Was it something I said?" He searched her face, worry wrinkling his forehead.

The band ended the last number and segued into a slower piece after the lead singer traded her fiddle for a mandolin. The soulful chords coupled with her softly trilling voice was hauntingly beautiful to Hilary.

"Yes and no. Dance with me."

She pulled him onto the middle of the dance floor. Surrounded by people, she didn't feel as conspicuous.

His arm around her waist, Dane pulled her close. Their hands intertwined as Hilary let the music guide her feet, her body swaying against Dane. Heat rose between them. Hilary felt a lightness in her with him near. The taste of his kiss was so close, yet—

"Well?" he said.

Hilary wanted to prolong this feeling. Everything was right with her world at the moment. Contentedness buoyed her. She wasn't plagued by someone else's dreams or expectations. No one was telling her how to feel or act. There was just Dane in front of her. Safe, strong, and sure Dane.

"What did I say to upset you? You can't throw something like that out there and expect me to forget—"

"She read the notes, Dane."

His feet slowed. "Notes?"

"Yes. The ones we wrote to each other on the bus yesterday?" She clenched her fist against his back. "I said some awful things about her."

"I don't remember anything that bad."

She drew back, wondering if he was serious.

"What did you say?" His voice grew louder. "That your sister-in-law refuses to acknowledge you're ready for a relationship after two years?"

Hilary hushed him. "It's not that. I made a commitment to her. And she's wondering now if I'm ready to throw it away for—"

"For me?"

Hilary shook her head. "It's more complicated than that. Besides, we barely know each other. Think about it from her perspective."

"It's not her call, Hilary. You're a grown woman."

"I know that. But you're the first man I've...been interested in since Will. She hasn't come to terms with it."

"So you like me?" he asked, grinning.

She sighed. While he was probably trying to inject a little humor into this, Hilary wasn't feeling it.

Dane seemed to sense it, hugging her close. "It's been two years. She should be happy for you."

"I don't want to hurt her."

He drew back, his gaze resting on her. "You're making this way more complicated than it needs to be."

Dane didn't seem to get it. Was she not being clear or was he choosing not to understand?

"I don't know how this will work, Dane."

"You mean seeing each other?" He stopped dancing.

Hilary tried to move him along again, but he stood rooted to the spot. "We're hundreds of miles apart. Jorie and I are trying to get this inn up and running. You have a farm too."

"So, you don't want to even try to see each other? I'm not asking for a commitment, you know." His arm around her waist loosened.

She rested her forehead against his shoulder and

inhaled that musky, woodsy scent that was all male. Hilary was going to miss that so much.

"I know that." She didn't want to talk about it anymore. All she wanted was to be held, to get carried away with the music, to feel his lips on hers again. "I don't want to say goodbye tonight."

"It doesn't have to be goodbye ever, Hilary."

The frustration was back in his tone. Hilary gazed up at him, looking for defeat there too. His gaze held hers for a moment as if waiting for words he wanted to hear. Words she couldn't say. Then he looked over her head towards the people on the dance floor as the corners of his mouth dipped.

Hilary turned around. Across the tent, Jorie held up a drink and motioned for her to come.

Hilary looked back at him. "What time do you leave in the morning?"

He still wouldn't look at her. "Early."

"Will I see you before I go?" She squeezed his hand, trying to get his attention again.

"Sure." He looked down at her. This time his expression was blank.

The music slowed as if on cue, like it was time for goodbyes. She slipped her hand from his.

"Okay. See you tomorrow then."

His brows raised.

Behind him, Jorie watched them intently.

Without a second thought, Hilary stood on tiptoes and took his face in both hands for one last kiss.

It was as if the contact brought him back to life. Dane's arms swept around her, one at her waist, the other encircling her back. It was so full of urgency and passion, it stopped her breath for a few seconds until spots appeared like they had that afternoon. His lips devoured hers, tasting and nibbling, hungry for more.

The music stopped, but the spinning in her head didn't. Her hands slid from his face to around his back, pulling him deeper into the kiss. He responded with a sound low in his throat as his hand moved to the back of her head. Oh, she didn't want this to stop. Not now, not ever.

With their first kiss, it astonished Hilary how much she missed the physical closeness with another man. She'd missed being touched and wanted. And now, Hilary knew it was this man she'd dream about long after they parted. She'd gotten a small taste of what the future might look like with Dane. There were so many things left to discover about him, to do together, to hope for.

His arms loosened around her. If Dane wasn't holding her, she might have trouble staying upright. Her body was a feather, light and without anchor. Deep breath. And another. Hilary stepped out of his embrace. She glanced again at Jorie, who was now sitting at one of the tables, glowering at them.

She touched her lips. Her lip balm was long gone.

Instead, her mouth felt swollen and bruised, but in a good way. Hilary smiled, even though Jorie sent imaginary daggers her way.

"I have to go." She reached to brush a stray lock of air away from his eye. "I'll text you."

Dane nodded. Even under the dim lighting, his face was obviously flushed. The skin on his neck rippled like he struggled to swallow.

Hilary patted down her hair as she made her way across the tent to Jorie. Since she'd seen their heated kiss, Hilary braced herself for Jorie's inevitable comment.

"Well, that was some make-out session." Jorie lounged in the chair, one leg crossed over the other, foot swinging.

"I'm going up to pack." Hilary paused beside her.

"No, sit with me. I have a drink for you," she said, pushing it toward her on the table.

"I'm not thirsty."

"All right," she said smoothly. Jorie cocked her head. "You know, I—"

Hilary couldn't stand there any longer. She wanted to sort through what Dane said about seeing each other again and concentrate on the lingering effects of his kiss. Jorie's babbling would diminish everything. In fact, she was sure whatever Jorie had to say would kill the mood, intentionally or not.

Chapter Seventeen

Hilary stood near the tiger maple credenza, drumming her fingers on its marble surface. She was anxious. There was no reason for it other than she didn't like flying, but even that wasn't so bad that it would affect her now. Next to her, Darcy tapped away on her keyboard.

Darcy squinted at the computer screen. "I'm so sorry to keep you waiting. These check out mornings during conferences are so hectic." She took out a book, flipped through a few pages, and then hit some buttons on her keyboard. Seconds later a receipt spit out of the printer next to her. Darcy handed it to Hilary.

"I hope you enjoyed the conference," she said, looking directly at Hilary, even though Jorie stood nearby, scrolling on her phone screen.

Hilary smiled. "I did very much. Thank you."

"I'm happy that you seemed to connect with so many people," Darcy said, her focus again on the computer. Hilary didn't miss the double meaning behind her words though. When Darcy looked back at her, her eyes flitted to Jorie before they rested on Hilary. "Especially some of the presenters."

Beside them now, Jorie sniffed loudly. "Dane Porter seemed to be an especially good resource." She smiled brightly, and Hilary couldn't help but notice how forced it looked.

Darcy closed her laptop. "You're lucky he stuck around a few extra days so you were able to pick his brain."

A few extra days? "What do you mean?" Hilary stopped tapping her fingers.

"He was supposed to leave on Wednesday morning. He extended his stay by two days."

"Why did he do that?" Jorie asked. "That must have cost a fortune. Speaking from experience, of course."

Darcy ignored Jorie and gave Hilary a pointed look. "I think he was worried about what he'd miss if he left early."

Hilary swallowed. The sense of melancholy she'd woken up with descended on her again like a shroud. It was even worse when she found out he'd left hours ago, practically in the middle of the night. Why didn't he tell her when she asked to see him this morning? Her texts to him went unanswered too. Maybe it was better ending their time together with that kiss. She couldn't count how many times she'd played it over in her head, committing it to memory. It had been perfect. Anyway, with Jorie's talent for showing up at inopportune times, who was to say there would have been a chance for a proper goodbye.

"He probably learned as much as we did by networking." Hilary played off Darcy's comment so Jorie wouldn't catch on. Hilary wasn't looking forward to the two-hour ride to Duluth, especially if Jorie lectured her again about focusing on the inn.

"Maybe, but I don't think that was it," Darcy said. She glanced at Jorie again, but she was busy tucking the receipt into her bag.

Hilary studied Darcy for a few seconds. Darcy smiled again. This time she seemed to say something with her eyes.

"I'm heading outside to lock up the cabins," Darcy said. "I'll help you with your bags if you'd like."

She didn't wait for an answer. She rolled Hilary's suitcase toward the side door, the wheels rumbling across the wood floor with Jorie trailing behind them.

Outside, milky clouds rolled across the sky. Hilary lifted her suitcase into the back of the Subaru wagon Jorie rented in Duluth. Hilary looked back at the inn, taking a mental picture of it. How different the week turned out. She'd arrived carrying resentment on her back like a load of bricks. Now she looked back on the week with a full heart. A full but conflicted heart.

Jorie was already in the driver's seat, buckling herself in.

Darcy laid a hand on Hilary's arm.

"I didn't want to say anything inside," she said, giving Hilary an envelope with the Blueberry Point Lodge logo in the upper-left corner. It was sealed. Darcy glanced toward Jorie. In a lower voice, she continued, "Sean took Dane and the others to the airport at four this morning. Dane asked me to give this to you."

Hilary stared dumbly at the envelope. He could write a letter but not answer her texts?

"Dane and I aren't lifelong friends, but I know him pretty well. He's not one to fall hard and fast for someone. He's very careful." Darcy's usual exuberance was tempered. She gave Hilary a soft smile. "He's worth whatever trouble you have to go through to make it work."

Whatever trouble you have to go through.

Hilary slipped the note into her pocket. "Thanks for letting me know."

Darcy dropped her hand from Hilary's arm. "Safe travels."

Inside the car, Jorie tuned in to a classic rock station. It played softly, Boston singing "More Than a Feeling." Hilary didn't want to listen to a song about regrets and watching someone walk away. She switched it off.

"I was listening to that." Jorie gripped the wheel with two hands as she pulled onto Highway 61.

Hilary leaned against the headrest. "I don't feel like listening to music now."

"What did Darcy say to you about Dane? I heard her say he left at four?"

"Yes, that's what she said."

"That's an ungodly hour," Jorie said, not taking her eyes from the road. Then, "I'm sorry."

"Sorry for what?"

"That you connected with someone who, under better circumstances, might be a great guy to get to know a little better."

"What's that supposed to mean?"

Jorie turned the music back on but kept the volume down. "He lives far away. Relationships are hard enough without adding hundreds of miles to the equation."

Hilary almost laughed aloud, but the anger welling up inside her drowned even a sarcastic comeback. Here Jorie was sympathizing with her, when for the last three days she took every chance to talk Hilary out of her interest in Dane. And what did Jorie know about long-distance relationships? She'd lived in the same house all her life and married her high school sweetheart.

"Did you forget Will and I met in college? That I lived in California during the two summers we dated before graduation? That I worked there for a year before we married and I moved to Redville?"

"No, I didn't," Jorie said. "All I'm saying is it takes a lot of energy, and you barely know him."

Hilary took the letter from her pocket and slipped a finger under the flap, opening it. What she knew about Dane she really liked. Why wasn't Jorie on her side?

"What's that?" Jorie asked.

"A letter from Dane."

Defiance surged in her. Let her wonder what it said. Hilary slipped the paper from the envelope. Dane's bold handwriting wasn't the neatest. The letter looked hastily written too. She took a deep breath.

Hilary -

First, I know this note is a poor substitute for a real goodbye. I know you would have gotten up to see me off at 4 a.m. if I told you, so I wanted to spare you that. The other reason is purely selfish and I hope you can at least understand. I would rather have the memory of last night, kissing you under the tent, than a rushed goodbye in the dead of night. That kiss was, well, it was something. I hope you're not too mad. Maybe you feel the same way. That's what I'm hoping.

She swallowed. So she was right. That kiss was a much better way to end the week. No words could have conveyed what their time together meant to him. Or to Hilary for that matter. Hilary continued reading:

I'm going to say this again so there's no misunderstanding. I would love to see you again. Clove isn't that far from Redville, less than a day's drive. But I think there are larger obstacles in the way than distance. If you feel like dealing with those challenges, I'll be your biggest cheerleader. But if not, I get it.

Yours,

Dane

Challenges.

Hilary looked over at Jorie. Her sister-in-law stared at the road ahead.

Jorie had been such an amazing help to Hilary. Strong, determined, never wavering in her belief that Hilary could get through losing Will. And while Jorie herself grieved terribly for him, Hilary never saw her break down. There weren't episodes of sobbing behind closed doors or tears brought on by a special song. Sometimes Hilary came out of her bedroom in the morning and caught Jorie staring at the framed photos in the hallway, visual reminders of the happy childhood she'd shared with her younger brother on the farm and the family vacations at the lake house. Jorie brought his name up in conversation a lot too. But Jorie wasn't one for emotional displays. She was too stoic.

Jorie glanced over at the note in Hilary's lap but was silent. If she was curious, Jorie didn't let on. Maybe Jorie learned a lesson after reading the flirty messages she and Dane shared the other day.

Hilary rested her forehead against the window, watching the landscape as they drove west. She sighed.

Clove and Redville *were* far apart.

The bed-and-breakfast would be operational by the

fall, September at the earliest.

There were recipes to test and marketing to worry about.

Maybe it was for the best.

"What is?" Jorie asked.

Oh, did she say that out loud? She closed her eyes momentarily and the memory of Dane's expression floated into her subconscious, the way he'd looked at her before they kissed last night.

"I'm thinking of all that needs to be done." She looked across at Jorie. "Now that I have some semblance of a timeline in my head. When will the contractors be finished?" The last she'd heard it would be within the month. Jorie and Tom coordinated the major work. When they were finished, Hilary would take over with decorating—painting, staining, uncovering furniture. A tiny ripple of excitement ran through her. Honestly, the idea of putting those rooms together was something she'd been looking forward to for months.

"Soon. Very soon." Jorie gave her a cheesy smile, reaching over to give Hilary a short pat on the leg. "I have a surprise for you."

"Oh yeah?"

Jorie nodded. "You're really going to love it."

Okay.

It was all going to work out. Her life would resume. Dane's too. It was a week they'd never forget. But one week wasn't long enough to build a future.

Chapter Eighteen

Several days of rain in Clove while Dane was away left the fields too soggy to work. The plants were at their peak, but harvesting had to wait for the sun to dry them out again. The workers were restless. Today they chose to sit underneath the two cottonwoods on the property, spitting sunflower seed casings into an empty plastic coffee container. That or singing at the tops of their lungs, their preferences running the gamut from Marty Robbins to Pearl Jam. There would be plenty of sun today. And humidity. Sweat broke out on Dane's forehead even before he left the house. He'd give the workers the go-ahead after lunch to get into the fields.

As much as the impromptu a cappella concert outside lifted his spirits, Dane preferred quiet. He hid out in the distillation shed, which he also used as his office. From his desk he listened to the tranquil sounds of the separation process taking place in the other room. Maria, a longtime family friend from the other side of the valley who ran her own profitable essential oils business online took care of his product lines. She was a self-starter and loved working independently. Sometimes her daughter Kelly came to help. Dane gave Maria free rein to try new products for the farm shop and the online store and considered her a good friend. She was also funny in a very understated way.

"I'm heading out for the day."

Maria stood in the door, leaning against the doorframe when Dane looked up. She'd startled him. He was lost in concentration, trying to find a mistake he'd made on an order spreadsheet.

He shook the mental cobwebs away. "I'm sorry. What?"

Maria crossed her arms. She was middle-aged with a weatherworn complexion and full head of premature white hair, which was always gathered at the nape of her neck. Maria lived in flannel shirts and polypropylene pants, no matter if it was twenty degrees or eighty. "I put in the last batch, so it'll be another two hours before it's finished."

He leaned back in his chair, using one hand to rake the hair from his forehead. "That's all right. I have nowhere to go."

"You work too hard," she said in a motherly tone.

"It's energizing."

"You've been quiet since you've come home. Is everything all right?" Her expression was sympathetic.

Dane closed his laptop and stood to stretch the kinks out of his back. He'd slept restlessly since coming home from the conference. It was catching up to him.

"It's nothing that harvest and a good night's sleep won't cure." Liar.

"If you say so. I'll see you tomorrow then." She turned to leave but stopped. "You might suggest they throw in gospel a little more often. Josiah has the best voice out there, and he only halfheartedly sings that other stuff."

Dane laughed. "I don't call what they're doing singing as much as yelling in harmony."

Maria pointed at him. "True."

"But I'll put the bug in someone's ear. See you, Maria."

After she left the building, Dane walked over to one of the tall windows overlooking the south field. At the height of bloom, the lavender fields were a surreal sight. He never tired of it. The acres of soft purple rows stretched toward the river and disappeared when the land gently sloped as it neared the banks. By the weekend this field would be cleared. Then cuttings would be shipped to retailers, crafters, processed into oil, and dried. Keeping the farm profitable took the expertise and time of many people. Yeah, he owned it, but he wouldn't fool himself. There was no way he could do it without a lot of help.

His phone beeped, a text coming through. Dane fished

it out of his pocket as a small burst of hope filled him. But when he read the text from his brother Ben, reminding Dane that he was flying into Boise on Sunday, that feeling faded as it had each time since last Saturday.

So far, Dane hadn't heard from Hilary. He promised himself he wouldn't text or call, even though he composed countless messages only to delete them. Still, he hoped once she read his note she would at least acknowledge it. Dane wondered if Hilary received the message at all until Darcy checked in with him yesterday, thanking him for helping with the conference and wondering if he was settled into his routine again. She brought up the note first. Dane wanted to know if Hilary had opened it right then. But she hadn't, which left Dane worried that Hilary misplaced it or worse, decided that confronting her sister-in-law was too great an obstacle to overcome now that Dane was out of the way.

He sat at the desk again, kicking up his feet, scrolling through the conference photos on his phone. It was here somewhere—yes, here it was. He and Hilary at the lighthouse on Friday morning, huddled together in the blanket. They'd stood to capture the lake in the background. Hilary inclined her head toward his, he'd hugged her closer, and their smiles were wide and genuine. Then they'd both blinked at the same time when the sun blinded them before Dane took the photo. That and a strand of Hilary's hair blew across Dane's face, landing under his nose like a silky mustache. Afterward,

Hilary laughed about the photo and asked him to forward that one too. It was the best one of all, she'd said.

Looking at the photo now, he smiled to himself, a soft laugh escaping as he studied their faces pressed together. Their time together had been too short. That was it. The connection they'd made wasn't made strong enough in a week. And Hilary felt too self-conscious once Jorie showed up. No, they hadn't spent enough time together to forge a bond even if he felt—-

Felt what?

Dane zoomed in on the photo. It surprised him, the way he felt. Dane realized he didn't have any reservations about taking a risk. Not with Hilary. His short marriage to Felicia blew up three years ago. Suffering through that kind of betrayal again terrified him. He promised himself he'd never be so blindsided again by another person, even going so far as to think he wouldn't bother for a long time. Yet here was Hilary. He'd known her a week and he was willing to risk it all.

Risk what exactly?

What did he feel? What was he willing to do?

Hilary's smile blazed up at him.

Dane went through his contacts and found Hilary's name. His finger hovered over her number. All he needed to do was call. Then he'd hear her voice and it would be like she wasn't hundreds of miles away but right next to him. So close.

No.

He wouldn't do that.

He'd written her the note and what happened?

Nothing. That was what happened. She was either so busy that calling him was low on her priority list or she didn't want to talk.

The number on his phone taunted him. He could check in, tell her he wondered if she was settled back in yet. And how was the progress on the B & B coming along? Keep it casual and light.

His curiosity battled with his insecurities. Maybe deep down he was afraid of facing rejection again or why else couldn't he call her right then? He wouldn't lie to himself. Yes, that was why he sat staring dumbly at his phone for the last fifteen minutes. Dane was scared. There was a certain risk after all; he lied to himself for denying it. His fear of losing the slim thread of hope outweighed his need to talk with her.

The ball lay squarely in her court, and that ball happened to be his note. No, he'd wait longer to hear from her. He'd pray that he did, but if for whatever reason Hilary chose not to reach out, Dane would accept it.

Dane slipped the phone into his jacket pocket. It hadn't been easy. But if Hilary chose to turn her back on him for good, what else could he do? It had been five days since he'd seen her. With each passing day, his hopes dimmed a little more.

Chapter Nineteen

J orie was big on surprises. She'd thrown surprise
birthday parties for Tom and Will. One for Cal's
sixtieth last October too. She told Hilary the best
part about throwing surprise events was that she
got a rush on the guest of honor's initial reaction. And
she loved the planning part, pulling out all the stops to
keep the secret.

I have a surprise for you, Jorie said on the way home
from the conference. And that was the last Hilary heard
about it until this morning. Today was the day, Jorie said
at breakfast, her excitement brimming. Hattie must have
sensed it. She clapped her hands, knocking over her bowl
of cereal, which scattered little wheat rings across the
floor.

"It won't take long," Jorie said. "I promise. I know
you're busy."

On hands and knees, Hilary soaked up the spilled milk with a rag. "Not so busy that I can't put it all aside for a bit. Did you ever make that appointment with the bank?"

Jorie brushed wheat loops into a dustpan with a hand broom. Still in her high chair, Hattie cheered them on. "Friday at nine," Jorie said.

Since coming home from the conference, Hilary spent the days reorganizing. She'd gone back to working on the vision boards for the bedrooms in the inn. She also drafted three short articles from ideas Dane helped her come up with after his presentation on content marketing. Keeping busy was easy now that she was home again. Her hectic schedule was a blessing in disguise. There was less time to dwell on what she missed. And she missed Dane; there was no denying it.

"I've got the rest," Jorie said, dumping cereal into the garbage can. "Go upstairs and get ready. I'll be waiting for you down here."

Her hair still damp, Hilary followed Jorie to the truck a short time later. Tom waited in the driver's seat with the engine on, grinning in his quiet, good-natured way. In the backseat, Hattie was pitching a fit for being subdued in her car seat this early in the day.

A plum-colored bandana floated into Hilary's lap.

"Put that on. Double it up so you can't see through it," said Jorie, smiling. "I know how you like to cheat."

"What? I should probably take offense at that, but I'm too excited." Hilary laughed and followed Jorie's orders, tying the fabric tight around her eyes. She couldn't even guess what Jorie had planned. "I hope this isn't too far or I'm going to get motion sickness."

"Not far at all."

They bumped along the uneven rural roads for a good ten minutes, Hilary guessed. She tried to map out in her mind the route Tom took. But there were too many turns, and after a few minutes queasiness took over. Hilary breathed deeply to calm her stomach.

"Okay, here we are," said Jorie.

"Good, because I'm about to lose my breakfast."

Gravel crunched under the truck's tires until Tom pulled to a stop.

Jorie led Hilary by the arm after they were out of the truck.

"Just another minute," Jorie said.

Hilary took baby steps. She didn't entirely trust Jorie not to lead her into something, not out of maliciousness but because Jorie's attention was always pulled in a million different directions. She missed things.

"Going up steps. Let's take it slow," said Jorie.

The hollow thud of wooden steps was a giveaway. They were at the Robillaud house. She recognized the fresh wood smell when they walked through the front door.

"Can I take this off yet?"

"A few more steps."

She didn't have the heart to tell Jorie she knew where

they were. She got so uptight about the littlest things sometimes.

Jorie tugged on her arm. "Okay. Stay here. I need to do one thing."

There was the sound of blinds being opened.

"I think we're ready."

Hilary slipped off the bandana.

Confusion clouded her reaction.

Hilary oriented herself by looking out the living room window for the road. That was how foreign her surroundings seemed at the moment. What threw her off the most was the furniture in front of her. The futon and oak entertainment she and Will bought together after their wedding, their first big purchase together, sat in this newly painted room instead of the farmhouse she shared with Cal, Jorie, Tom, and sweet little Hattie. There was other furniture she didn't recognize set in groupings for easy conversation and games or something else guests might want to do in a spacious common area of an inn.

Speechless, Hilary walked into the kitchen, now fitted with the dark wood cabinets, white tile floor, and a cherry red Aga stove she and Jorie decided on months ago.

"I decided to have the contractors just take the walls down to the studs and put in drywall here. I figured there was no sense in getting a brand-new kitchen without getting brand-new walls."

Hilary turned a complete circle, taking in the gorgeous kitchen. Gone were the plaster walls she'd diligently stripped of wallpaper layers and painted last fall. What was the point of all the work if Jorie already secured money for these major renovations?

"I don't even... I have no words." Hilary looked around, thinking the mirage would clear and the half-finished house with exposed lathe walls and worn woodwork would appear again.

"Isn't it amazing? Tell me you love it."

"Didn't we decide *not* to put up new drywall because of costs?"

Jorie shrugged. "Tom and I scraped a little more money together. Plus, the drywall guy gave me a great quote once I told him the extent of the project. It was much lower than I thought it would be."

All Hilary heard was "I." This was Jorie's project, not theirs.

"I thought this would take months to finish," Hilary said in a measured tone. She rubbed her neck, feeling the heat of shock and frustration there. "I thought we were working on this together."

There were even utensils in a salt-glazed crock on the counter, cordless blinds installed over the new nine-paned window above the sink. Braided rugs, placemats, and a shiny chrome-and-black espresso machine on a rolling metal cart too. The inn looked ready to host their first guest that night.

Jorie leaned against the counter, crossing her arms. She looked at the floor, taking her time to answer.

"Honestly, I didn't want to wait anymore. And we did do it together. I just hastened the process."

"This was a huge thing to keep from me, Jorie."

Jorie's expression turned sympathetic. "I thought you were losing interest. You haven't been over here in months. I figured if I got it up and running, you might get excited about it again."

"I *am* excited about the inn. Just because I don't talk about it constantly doesn't mean I've given up on the idea." Hilary drew a deep breath. A knot formed in her chest. That wasn't entirely truthful. *Excitement* wouldn't be the word she'd use. But how could she ever talk to Jorie about her doubts, especially after all this?

Jorie took her through the rest of the house. She couldn't be faulted for the decorating decisions she'd made. The place was so inviting, a bed-and-breakfast worthy of a magazine spread. Six bedrooms, some named after the apple varieties in the orchard on the property, were the picture of tranquility. The Cortland boasted deep reds and dark woods with a four-poster bed. A flower garden quilt, mint-green walls, and white billowy curtains with pom-pom fringe charmed her in The Granny like she'd imagined. Green was her favorite color after all. It had been Will's too. She and Jorie spent hours poring over magazines and color samples. Yes, the color schemes in the rooms were the same, but the details were all Jorie. Hilary had merely been along for the ride while

Jorie did most of the work. This felt like Jorie's dream. Jorie and Will's dream.

Hilary walked into the light-filled room, leaving Jorie leaning against the wall in the hallway. Her footsteps on the wood floor echoed, as there was only a bed and chest of drawers in the room. She ran her hand over the oak chest and sighed. A sudden sense of loneliness gnawed at her stomach. It was as if everyone around her had taken two steps forward and she stood rooted to the spot. Hilary felt paralyzed.

"It feels like I'm apologizing a lot lately," Jorie said quietly. "I didn't mean to step on your toes. I want you to be happy here."

"No, you're right. I haven't been as excited as you about it. Maybe it's been hard for me to visualize up until now." Hilary turned to Jorie. "It's beautiful. Really."

"So, you're not mad?"

Hilary swallowed. "No. Not mad at all."

She walked over to the window and looked out across the property. It was a few acres of cottonwoods, maples, and one gnarled oak tree. The footprints of long-ago perennial gardens were scattered on the lawn. Hilary would love to revive them. Beyond the lawn, the orchard stood. They'd counted roughly eighty trees. There was work to do there too. Lots of pruning. Come September, the trees would be laden with pinpoints of red and yellow. So many apples.

The memory of her and Dane during their unexpected meeting that night in the kitchen at the inn swam up from her subconscious. They'd been talking about pie. Her mother's cranberry apple recipe to be exact. He'd tried talking her into capitalizing more on these apples, maybe making pies to sell commercially, which had never been on her radar. Sure, she loved to bake, but getting licenses and being subjected to inspections terrified Hilary. He'd told her to think about it. Selling food wasn't as hard as she thought.

Hilary returned to her room that night, thinking about pies. Her mother was a pie master, and Hilary inherited a good smattering of talent too from helping her in the kitchen. There wouldn't be a shortage of apples with an orchard in the backyard, that was for sure. Hilary convinced herself to start experimenting with her mother's pie recipes. Somewhere in the attic, amongst the boxes Hilary moved from home before she married Will, was her mother's pie bible. She hadn't thought about until that night in the kitchen with Dane. Hilary loved the thing, a messy, stained compilation of handwritten recipes collected over years of culinary experiences. Her great-grandmother had even passed down some of those recipes. Hilary thought about the recipe for lavender apple pie that she'd mentioned to Dane. She smiled. She'd never baked with lavender, but maybe it was time to try.

"Hilary?"

She startled. "Sorry. Just admiring the view of the orchard." Hilary turned away from the window.

"Okay, good. For a minute, I thought you... never mind," she said, shrugging. "I'm glad you're not upset."

Hilary walked across the room again. She glanced at the flower pattern on the quilt. The petals were a cheery mix of greens, yellows, and pinks. And lavender.

"Why would I be mad? Now I get to concentrate on the marketing plans. And testing recipes."

Jorie stuck her finger in the air. "About recipes. I have some ideas for—"

"Jorie, please stop." She wasn't about to surrender that task to Jorie.

"You're right. I've taken over enough."

It wasn't often Jorie uttered those words. In fact, it might be a first, Hilary mused. She'd write it down somewhere. For posterity.

Downstairs, Jorie led her through the rooms that hadn't been finished. There was still work to do in the front rooms and the library, painting, refinishing the woodwork on the built-in shelves, rehanging doors that had been stashed in the attic.

"What do you say we tackle the rest over the weekend? Tom called dibs on the shelving. You and I will have the painting done in no time if I can get Della to watch Hattie on Saturday and Sunday."

"Sounds like a plan." Hilary eyed the paint cans, ready and waiting, in the corner of the library.

Jorie sighed. "It's finally going to happen." She grinned, hitching her shoulders up to her ears, then dropping them again.

"Yes, it is," Hilary said. She headed toward the door now that they'd toured the whole house.

"Tom and I can't stop talking about it. I so wish Will could see this. He would love that we're doing this together."

Together.

Funny, she thought they were in it together too. But the work upstairs and in the kitchen didn't mesh with Jorie's claim. Jorie left Hilary out of the plans. What else would happen without Hilary's knowledge, all in the name of togetherness?

LATER THAT AFTERNOON, HILARY VENTURED UP to the attic while Hattie napped and Jorie ran to the hardware store in town. The space was an unfinished, vaulted behemoth of an area, all exposed beams and arched windows clouded with grime. In the winter, frost expanded into snowflake patterns where the roofing nails poked through the planks overhead. It was peaceful. If money was abundant, she'd insulate it and make it her bedroom, private and cozy.

Hilary shuffled around the boxes stacked three high among dining room chairs no longer in use, Christmas decorations, and a standing Victrola pushed as far back as it could go under the eaves. She diligently arranged her belongings into a neat stack when she'd moved to the farm. Time added a solid layer of dust to the pile, and she coughed as she lifted off the top box. Of course the one she needed was at the bottom.

Brushing off one of the dining chairs, Hilary sat. She lifted the lid from the plastic tub. So many memories. High school yearbooks, newspaper clippings from the year her volleyball team went to state, hand-crocheted coasters, a program from the Chicago musical she attended with her grandmother in eighth grade had been tucked away, waiting for her to reacquaint herself like an old friend. She didn't realize she was grinning until her cheeks started to ache.

And there it was—her mother's pie bible. The cover, a fuchsia cross-hatch pattern on contact paper, caught her eye. She pulled it from the bottom of the box. Little dust eddies swirled in the air in front of her as she brushed the cover off with her hand before she opened the book.

The pages had grown a little brittle with age. Her mother's precise writing was easy to read, as unpretentious as the recipes. Apple Pear Ginger pie. Coconut Macadamia. Lemon Hazelnut. Sometimes she included a photo clipped from the pages of a magazine. An amateur artist, her mother liked to sketch too. Crust designs and little bird shapes populated the pages too. The book was a treasure.

Hilary sat hunched over the book, slowly turning pages, taking it all in.

And here it was—lavender apple pie.

The recipe was simple enough. It sounded amazing. Now she'd need to hunt down some lavender. She might know just the person to ask.

Hilary fished her phone out of her back pocket and snapped a photo of the recipe. Then she scrolled through her messages, finding his name right away among the three texts she'd sent since she came home five days ago. What an exciting life she led. A real social butterfly she was.

While she typed out the message, Hilary caught herself full-on grinning again.

Have you ever tried apple lavender pie?

Chapter Twenty

🙣

The goats congregated in the barn earlier than usual, sensing rain was on the way. That meant Gertie, the affectionate matriarch of the herd, pressed herself against Dane's side as he tried to clean out the small stall inside the barn before supper. She nuzzled into his pockets, swatted him with her backside, and was a general sweet nuisance while he cleaned.

"Maria, take this please."

Dane passed Maria his phone. He'd learned not to carry it on him when he tended the goats. Gertie smeared it with silage in her search for treats. Another goat slipped it out of his back pocket once, thinking it a snack. So the phone stayed outside the corrals.

"They seem more ravenous than usual. Have you not been taking care of my girl?" Maria said, setting his phone on the wooden table beside her. She reached over the fence to scratch Gertie between her ears.

"Please. These beasts are more spoiled than toddlers at Christmas."

Gertie was Maria's favorite. Maria followed Dane to the barn earlier with a baggie filled with corn kernels and sliced apples. The other goats would compete with Gertie for the treats, and they'd get some too. But Gertie stood head and shoulders above the rest, easily craning her neck between the slats of the top two rails.

Dane leaned the rake against the outside of the stall and picked up the bucket of alfalfa mixture for the goats' trough. Gertie met him at the gate again, smelling more food coming her way.

His phone dinged.

Dane tipped the bucket to empty its contents into the feeder.

"Who's Hilary?" asked Maria.

The handle almost slipped out of his hand. He tossed the empty bucket aside and was through the gate and at Maria's side in two long strides. He snatched his phone from the cart before she read any more. Maria loved to gossip almost as much as she loved Gertie.

"Just someone I know."

Maria took an exaggerated step backward and held up her hands in surrender. "Obviously. I don't think you get many texts from strangers. Don't let me get in your way or anything."

"Sorry. I…it's something from the conference. I've been waiting for this person to get back to me."

"You've never been a good liar, you know. Your ornery brothers, yes. But I could always read the truth in your eyes."

"Give me a break." Dane pressed his lips together, annoyed. She liked teasing him, always had. Most times he took it. But today was different. The cart he used to pull the heavy bunches from the fields lost a wheel, so they'd loaded up the wheelbarrows instead, which took forever. Two of his workers went home sick an hour into the day. And more rain was coming tonight. This message was the bright spot of his day—his week actually—and he wasn't going to let Maria take that away from him.

"She must be pretty special. I haven't seen you move that fast since I watched you run the hundred-meter dash in high school."

"Maria, I didn't run track. I played baseball."

She snapped her fingers. "That's right. Rafe was the sprinter."

He gave her a sidelong glance. "You knew that. And I told you it's business. You're trying to rile me up."

Maria snickered. "Like that's even possible. I can finish up here—"

The sound of her voice trailed off as soon as Dane saw Hilary's name on the screen. He did a mental fist pump and opened his phone.

Have you ever tried apple lavender pie? she asked.

Huh.

No, he hadn't. That might be a little weird to admit as a lavender farmer, but he wasn't a big dessert guy. He weighed his response. Should he mention his reservations about combining his favorite fruit with an herb he equated with soap and body lotion? If he gave her a simple "no," that might shut down the conversation too quick. Maybe this was an invitation of some kind. Was she proposing a pie-tasting date?

Stop thinking so much and answer the text, you idiot.

He started typing and backtracked a few times, second-guessing himself.

No, but it sounds awesome, he responded. He was such a liar.

Her reply came back immediately. *Maybe you can be my guinea pig if you ever come for a visit.*

Wait—what? So it *was* an invitation. He took a deep breath, nervous about blowing an opportunity.

"Hello?"

He looked up. Maria braced herself against the corral, shaking her head.

"Some business contact," she said, grinning.

"Okay, fine. She's a woman I met at the conference. We hit it off. She lives in Redville, Idaho."

"Where's that?"

"About five hundred miles to the east."

"Do you have plans to see each other?"

Dane held the phone out and pointed at it with his other hand. "That's what I'm working on here, Maria."

She chuckled. "Okay. I can take a hint. I'll see you in the morning."

He tore his attention away from his phone for a second. "Wait, Maria."

She turned back. "Yes?"

"Thanks for sticking around today. For helping with the field."

Maria gave him an easy smile. "You're welcome. I bet you forgot I'm useful for more than just mixing oil."

"Not at all. If anything, you keep things rolling around here."

"You're just saying that because you want me to go." She stuck her hands in her back pockets. "I hope she's worthy of you."

Dane smiled. "She is. But I have to convince her to take a chance on me."

Maria's face brightened. "Give me her number. I can twist her arm."

"Goodbye, Maria."

She turned on her heels and waved to him over her shoulder without another word.

His full attention turned back to the conversation-in-progress. Where was he? Oh yeah, that invitation.

Are you inviting me to Redville? he typed, this time without hesitation, but gritting his teeth while his fingers flew across his phone.

The little dots appeared underneath his reply as Hilary worked on her answer. He waited, his heart beating against his shirt. In front of him, Gertie and her crew ate noisily while casting wary glances at him.

A new message popped up.

Maybe. I need some lavender though. I want to make this pie. And, well, you're the lavender guy.

I am indeed the lavender guy, he mused. It had a superpower ring to it. He should put that on a tee shirt.

His phone dinged again.

Can you send some? I'll pay for shipping of course.

It was a no-brainer. He'd put it in the mail tomorrow.

Another message came even before he had a chance to answer.

I don't expect freebies just because I have connections—ha!

Dane sighed and typed a reply.

Send me your address and I'll ship it out tomorrow.

Dane didn't want the conversation to end, but he didn't want to sound needy either. Her invitation wasn't really a serious one, but maybe this was enough for now. Taking it slow, he'd check in with her in a few days to see if the lavender came. *If* he didn't hear from her first.

Chapter Twenty-One

Fifteen minutes passed since the receptionist at Redville Community Bank led her and Jorie to one of the back offices. Hilary was restless. They were there to finalize a loan extension to finish last-minute details at the inn. Their loan officer, Beth Ontiveras, crossed in front of the glass window of the inner office no less than a half dozen times, a thick manila file pressed against her chest. If that wasn't annoying enough, Hilary's chair was uncomfortable. The wooden arms cut into the sensitive part of her forearms, so she grew increasingly more irritated each time the loan officer passed by in the hallway. Hilary slumped against the seat back, sighing, until the tone from an incoming text caught her attention. She leaned forward to pull it from her back pocket, but Jorie's hand was on her arm.

"Can you hold off until the meeting is over? I'm sure he can wait."

Hilary was about to let it go, but Jorie's reference to "he" made her freeze. And it was the biting tone too. Jorie assumed only one person in the world would text her. It wasn't a stretch, but still.

"You mean Dane."

Jorie nodded impatiently. "Who else?"

"We're just waiting. I'll put it away when Beth comes back."

Hilary looked down at her phone. Dane joked about booking a room at their bed-and-breakfast if only for a chance to see her. A giggle escaped Hilary before she could stop it. She pressed the back of her hand to her mouth before sending back a quick reply.

I told you the room would be pro bono if you give us a good review, she texted back.

Dane sent her a message earlier that morning to check if the lavender arrived. The box came yesterday afternoon via express mail. The scent permeated through the box even before she'd cut through the packing tape. Inside, a glass jar of dried buds sat nestled inside bubble wrap and purple tissue paper. She lifted the tissue to her nose, inhaling the lavender scent. Either Dane spritzed the inside of the box with oil or her brain conjured its sweetness before she unscrewed the jar lid. Hilary couldn't imagine what his farm smelled like when the fields were in bloom. She'd done a little snooping yesterday. Lavender Lane Farm had a gorgeous website and according to it, the fields were in full color now. She bet it was heaven for the senses.

The ding of another message snapped her out of the daydream.

I'll leave a good review even if I don't book one of your rooms, Dane texted.

She sent a shocked emoji. *What will you base your review on then?*

Her pulse thrummed in her neck. Hilary thought about excusing herself so she could hide in the restroom and keep this conversation going. But Beth came back into the office then, foiling her plan.

Dane's text popped up. *Your smile. That kiss.*

Her mouth went dry. She read the words again and a mental image of them locked in an embrace on the dance floor during their last night together paralyzed her. His lips on hers had been amazing, a feeling her body responded to even now just thinking about it.

"I'm not joking," Jorie said, patting Hilary on her knee. "C'mon. Eye on the ball," she whispered as Beth sat down again across the desk.

Hilary stared at the spot on her knee where Jorie touched her. Silently, she fumed. It was something a parent would do to a misbehaving child. She glanced up at Jorie, but her sister-in-law had already scooted her chair closer to the desk to look over the paperwork with Beth.

Minutes later, they walked out of the bank. Hilary planned to stop by the bakery on their way out of town. She'd been craving a cinnamon roll since coming back from the conference, but now she wanted to head home, her head full of numbers, deadlines, and resentment.

"You're awfully quiet," Jorie said, hitching her bag onto her shoulder as they crossed the parking lot.

Hilary chewed on her lip. She caught her reflection in the car window before she opened the door and frowned. Her sour mood was written all over her face.

"I don't talk for the sake of talking. There's nothing to say."

"You're mad," Jorie said.

Hilary buckled herself in, started the car, and then leaned her head against the seat. She waited for Jorie to stop fidgeting. Her head pounded and she was hungry. She'd skipped a full breakfast, opting for only a Greek yogurt since she'd written down the wrong time for the meeting. It wasn't her fault though. She'd written it down correctly, but then Jorie rescheduled without telling her. But that wasn't the real reason her mood tanked.

Jorie's innocent expression told Hilary she was clueless as to what upset her.

Hilary nodded. "You could say I'm a little irritated."

"I didn't expect the meeting to last that long. And we can totally shorten the term of the loan by paying it off early."

"That's not it, Jorie."

Jorie looked at her and blinked. "Well, what is it then?"

Hilary chewed the inside of her lip, stewing. Starting an argument was not her intention, but she was sick of it. All of it. The assumptions, the orders, the treatment like she was an inferior member in her own home, incapable of making the simplest decisions like who to text.

"I don't like being told to put my phone away like I'm a teenager at the dinner table."

"Oh that."

"No. Not *oh that*. And you used a tone when you implied it was Dane I was talking to."

"Weren't you?"

"Yes. So what?"

"I didn't think it was an appropriate time is all."

Hilary gave a short bark of a laugh. "You never think it's the right time to talk to Dane."

"Hilary, you've known this guy for less than a month. Don't you think you're in this too deep too fast?"

"Who are you comparing us to?" Her voice rose sharply. "Honestly, I feel like you're a little too vested in my relationships."

"You haven't had any relationships since...Will. This is the only one. I want you to be careful."

"Why can't you be happy for me?"

Jorie stared out the front window. "I don't know. I can't help but wonder where our plans fall into this. Don't forget who this is for."

"How can I forget when you remind me all the time?"

Jorie grimaced. "I'm sorry, but he was my brother." Her voice was barely above a whisper.

"And he was my *husband!*" The words erupted from Hilary, ringing her ears. A red haze seeped into her vision. How dare Jorie use Will to guilt her again.

Jorie gasped. Her eyes grew blurry as she looked at Hilary, and then Jorie buried her face in the crook of her arm, the most awful sounds filling the car. Hilary wasn't sure if they were sobs or if Jorie was hyperventilating.

"Jorie?"

The wailing didn't let up. Hilary looked outside the car, positive that anyone nearby would hear the commotion even with the windows rolled up. She reached across the seat to tentatively rest her hand on Jorie's shoulder, but Jorie twisted away. Unemotional, stoic Jorie was in the midst of a major meltdown, the first Hilary had ever seen.

Hilary touched her again, rubbing her arm this time, but Jorie pulled it against her side. Even as she tried comforting her, Hilary fumed. The unfairness of using Will's memory to manipulate her made Hilary entertain thoughts she never imagined having with regards to Jorie and the farm. Her anger but also sadness intertwined, burning in her throat, steeping like an ill-tasting brew while Jorie let go of all the pent-up emotion she'd hoarded for years.

Hilary looked over at Jorie again. She leaned against

the window, still crying into her shirtsleeve. This made sense though. In terms of grieving, Hilary had been efficient. In the months after Will's death, she folded inward, confining herself to her room to sleep, cry, and stare out the window at the vast fields of Larkin Farms, fields Will should have been plowing, planting, and harvesting over the course of the year. After one particularly bad day last March, when Cal and Tom brought the planter out of the shed, Hilary broke down. Jorie and Hattie were at a doctor's appointment in town. Alone in her room, she raged how unfair it was for Will to die. Poor Rowdy stood outside her room, scratching at the closed door. When Hilary let him in, Rowdy lay himself across her body on the bed and softly whined as she cried. That was the last day she'd cried. Her well had run dry it seemed.

On the contrary, Jorie sat in the front row during the funeral with her arm around Hilary, staring expressionless at the casket. She'd been the one to receive people during the visitation while Hilary spent more time in the funeral director's office with the lights turned off than she did amongst the other mourners. Aside from the initial news of Will's accident, Jorie didn't shed one tear in front of Hilary. She talked about him constantly, but never cried. Until now.

At last, Jorie opened the glove compartment, dug out a fast-food napkin, and honked into it.

"I miss him," Jorie said. She buried her nose in

another napkin, and a fresh round of sobs shook her shoulders.

"I know. I do too."

"I guess I'm afraid," Jorie said, her voice raspy.

Jorie afraid? What was more incredible—that Jorie feared something or that she actually admitted it?

Hilary studied her hands in her lap. She didn't like seeing Jorie like this. For so long, Jorie had been an anchor holding the family together, helping Hilary feel grounded again. The roll reversal caught her off guard.

"What are you afraid of?"

She crumpled up the napkins and grabbed another. "I don't want to do this all alone. It was really going to be something special with us working together—you, me, and Will. Now I'm not even sure you want to be a part of it anymore."

"Of course I do."

But did she? If the last two weeks were an indication, Hilary should have rethought her words. She resented being sent to the conference alone. Then finding Jorie took over much of the work at the house without her help added to her frustration. And each time Jorie butted in between her and Dane, well, the pendulum swung in favor of distancing herself from Jorie and the project. At least for the near future. As much as she hated the idea of hurting Jorie, it was time to be honest. With Jorie and herself.

She took Jorie's hand, hoping to soften the blow Jorie would surely feel.

"No...wait. That's not entirely true, Sis." Hilary couldn't look at her until she'd gotten what she wanted to say off her mind. "I don't want to *not* be involved, but maybe I need to step back a little."

Jorie nodded and started to sniffle again.

"I wish I could say this without hurting you, but it's been driving me crazy. This was Will's dream. It was mine too while he was still here. Now that he's not, I feel like I'm just going through the motions."

"I thought being involved would help you move on." Jorie shook her head. She dabbed at her eyes with her sleeve.

"Not really. I think it's not letting me move on. I need to do something different. At least for the time being. Get off the farm. Maybe take a vacation alone."

What Hilary wanted to do most of all was talk with Dane, hear his voice. She dreamed of him last night, the third time since she'd come home from the conference. There were times during the day where his face would swim to the forefront of her mind and it would literally stop her in her tracks. She kept looking at the time, calculating what they had been doing together during that weekday at the conference. From the time he picked her up at the Duluth airport to their goodbye kiss, Hilary replayed every hour in her mind. What she wouldn't do to go back there.

Jorie looked at her through watery eyes. "And reconnect with Dane."

"I'm not sure about that." *Oh, but she was.* Didn't she decide to be truthful?

Jorie touched her hand. "He'd be good for you, Hil. You two seemed very happy together."

"But there's the distance thing." Hilary picked at a nail, considering Jorie's blessing. She'd hoped for this, but Hilary couldn't shake her concern about Jorie thinking she was being deserted.

"What's a few hundred miles?" Jorie wadded up the sodden napkins and tucked them into her pocket. "It'll work itself out if it's meant to be."

"Jorie, please don't think I'm leaving you to figure everything out on your own. I still want to be involved." She shrugged. "But I don't know what I want *right now*. I still miss working in the schools too."

"Don't let us hold you back. You've suffered enough and need to lead your own life. Tom and I are capable of running this."

Hilary snorted. "Which means you'll give orders and he'll follow them."

"If he knows what's good for him." She chuckled, then groaned and slumped against the seat. "Please tell me this doesn't mean I have to figure out social media and marketing by myself."

"No worries. That's the fun part. I've got the plan for the rollout almost finished anyway."

Jorie pressed her palms together. "Thank goodness."

As they drove through downtown Redville on the way home, relief almost spilled out in happy tears. Hilary swallowed the lump sitting at the back of her throat and slipped on her sunglasses so Jorie couldn't see wetness brimming at the corners of her eyes. Finally she felt light, free from the burden of the lie she'd held on to for so long.

Chapter Twenty-Two

❧❀❧

Dane pulled next to the garage and shut off the truck's engine. Three hours at Clove Autobody that afternoon and four hundred dollars later, Dane cursed himself for not selling the piece of junk earlier in the spring. He'd list it online as soon as he got around to writing an ad. It was one more task to add to his growing list, all because of this never-ending rain.

He sat there, watching rivulets of water run down the windshield, putting off the inevitable dash to get inside and away from the rain. There were only a few vehicles in the farm visitor lot now. Dane wasn't surprised since the weather had been miserable since yesterday. June and July were the busiest months because the fields were in full color, summer vacations in high gear, and the farm store was fully stocked. Maria kept revolving orders with the local suppliers of handmade chocolates, beeswax products, and the braided wool rugs from Patsy Detmiller at Rag Bag Studios down the road. Maria's oils sold out faster than she could stock them. But nothing was moving today.

He pulled the hat brim lower as he opened his door and trotted across the lot with rain stinging his face. His boots slopped through puddles on the way to the enclosed porch at the back of the house. Inside, he stopped, the screen door snapping behind him.

Maria, Jesse, and the others sat around the screened room in lawn chairs, digging into plates of pie. The smell of freshly brewed coffee hung in the air.

Dane shook off his cap. "How come no one told me there was a party this afternoon?"

Maria set her plate down on the table beside her. Next to it was an empty pie plate and two more full pies.

"It was a last-minute one. Want a slice? It's amazing."

Dessert didn't usually grab his attention, but this looked like a decent apple pie. Add a cup of coffee to the equation and this impromptu gathering might lighten his sour mood. "Make it a good-sized one." He unfolded another lawn chair and joined their circle.

"How's the truck?" Jesse asked, a piece of crust clinging to his lower lip. Dane pointed to his own mouth before Jesse got the message and licked it away.

"It's working for now. New air compressor. But the brake lines are showing wear. George says it's only a matter of time before they need replacing. It's been something new every month for a while now."

Jesse rubbed his fingers together. "Ouch."

"No kidding. Time to start shopping." Dane took his first taste of the pie, closing his eyes as the pastry practically disintegrated in his mouth. "Man, this is good."

Maria smiled. "Coffee?"

"I'd love some."

Maria went into the kitchen and returned with a steaming mug. She set it on the table beside him.

Dane looked outside. "I'm hoping this rain lets up tonight like the reports say it will. Then we can finish the last field the day after tomorrow if it's dry enough."

One of the other guys, Ed Searle, a forty-something welder who helped around the farm between jobs, piped up. "If we get the high winds, maybe it'll dry overnight."

"Doubt it," Jesse said.

While Ed and Jesse debated the probability of harvesting tomorrow, Dane studied the next forkful of pie. He was pretty sure this was the best pie he'd ever tasted. For his second bite, Dane savored it, letting it sit on his tongue while he tried to distinguish its uniqueness. Across the table, Maria's grin grew wider when he caught her eye.

He scooped another piece onto his fork and pointed it at her.

"What's up with you? I haven't seen you smile this much since the last time you had the week off."

Maria chuckled. "That's so not true. I'm just getting a kick out of watching you romance that slice of pie."

"What did you put in here? It has a little kick to it."

"It's lavender," Maria said, arching a brow. "Lavender apple. And I didn't make them."

"Well, where did they—"

He froze, the fork hovering in front of his mouth.

"Did you say lavender apple?" It hit him like a lightning bolt.

Maria nodded, smiling like a bobblehead clown. "I did."

The pie slipped off the fork and landed on his shoe. He stared at her, his thoughts suddenly as pureed as apple filling. "Did she bring the pies herself?"

"Who?" Jesse asked, his eyes darting between Maria and Dane.

Ed whacked him with his cloth napkin. "Dane's lady friend, you dolt. Hilary, right?"

"Yes." Maria lifted her chin toward the direction of the barns. "Kelly took her for a tour. She asked to see the goats."

Dane nodded, his mouth dry.

"She showed up about an hour ago, looking for you," Maria continued. "I—"

But Dane didn't stick around to hear Maria finish the sentence. He was outside again, jogging in the direction of the goat barn, not feeling the stinging rain this time, his unbuttoned jacket flapping behind him.

He pulled open the door and blinked, his eyes adjusting to the darkness. At the far end of the barn, silhouetted against the opening to the pasture, were two figures in hooded raincoats standing at the inside corral.

"Surprise," Kelly whispered when she met him halfway down the aisle. Maria's daughter wore the same impish grin as her mother. "I'll let you finish the tour," she said over her shoulder as she headed out of the barn.

Dane stood there, looking at Hilary, who seemed frozen in place too. He couldn't quite believe she was here. Slowly, he walked toward her as if a sudden movement might cause her to fade away like an apparition. She pushed off her hood when he came closer.

"Hello," she said. Her eyes, brightened by the dim light, swept over him before she focused again on his face. There were the fleeting dimples. He missed them. Her expression showed a mixture of emotions fighting for control.

"I had no idea you were coming." There was a tremor in his voice too. Dane cleared his throat. "I would have been here." He stopped within an arm's length of her.

A tremulous smile lit her face. "I didn't want to get in the way if you were busy. And I was a little nervous. I was going to leave the pies and call you from the road."

He let out a short bark. "That would have killed me if I didn't get to see you." He took a step closer. The skin at the base of her throat rippled as she inhaled.

"This is on the way to my sister's," she said. "I'm going to stay with her for a while."

Dane reached for her hand. It was soft and warm and she squeezed his when they touched.

"Is everything all right?" he asked. She looked happy but he wondered if there was trouble with Jorie.

"Everything's fine," she said, looking him up and down again. "I forgot how good you look when you're wet."

He chuckled while he pulled his shirt collar up to wipe the rain from his face. A surge of warmth spread through him. Hilary was here. She'd come to see him.

"I'm taking a little 'me' time. It's been a while since I went home." She tilted her head, her eyes searching his face.

He wanted to ask her what changed, making her want to leave the farm in Redville when it was almost crunch time for opening the inn. What had Jorie thought about her taking off? Did Jorie know that Hilary and her traveling pie shop would stop to see him? These and other questions popped into his mind as he stared at her.

"And I've missed you," she said, taking the last step to close the space between them. Hilary's other hand traveled up his arm to rest on his shoulder. Her bottom lip quivered. "A lot. Texting wasn't doing it for me anymore."

That was all he needed to know.

Dane cupped her face in both hands. "I missed you too," he whispered. "So much."

The kiss was like a slow-motion clip. Hilary leaned toward him. Their lips met with perfect choreography. He closed his eyes and reveled in the delicate touch of her mouth against his. Dane half expected cheers to erupt or a choir of angels to burst into song, but the buzzing in his ears would have drowned it out. Her lips were butter soft and moist, more tantalizing than he imagined in his daydreams since they'd seen each other last. His arms went around her, pressing her against his chest, and Hilary responded by conforming to his body like a puzzle piece. Behind them, the goats bumped against the corral fence, making soft snorting noises, oblivious to the significance of the moment in their quest for food.

They'd have to wait.

HE AND HILARY SAT INSIDE THE SCREENED porch long after everyone scattered, listening to the rain pound the metal roof and sharing an impromptu dinner of baby greens and other vegetables from the garden, a good balance after eating more than half a pie. Dane took her plate to the kitchen when they'd finished, then came back onto the porch, turning on some bluegrass before he sat down again. He'd been listening to it ever since the band played at Blueberry Point Lodge since it took him back to that night. Dane scooted his chair closer to Hilary so their knees touched.

"I really debated about telling you I was coming," Hilary said, wrapping the gauzy blue scarf tighter around her neck. The blue made the color of her hair all the more richer. It was cooler than usual for early July. The rain brought a welcome cold front on its heels. Dane had since ditched the flannel he wore earlier, but goosebumps rose on his arms from the chill. Or maybe it was the present company affecting him.

He shook his head. "Had I known, I would have put off the truck appointment another day."

She looked down at her lap, playing with the scarf's fringe, and laughed. "I kind of wondered if you wanted to see me."

"You're joking, right?"

She lifted her shoulder. "But when I walked into your store and Maria found out who I was, that made me feel better." Hilary smiled and wrinkled her nose. Dane was so charmed by her expression he momentarily lost the question that came to mind. "She's funny," Hilary said.

"Sometimes to a fault. What did she say to you?" Dane didn't think he ever mentioned Hilary by name to Maria. Then he remembered. She'd seen Hilary's name pop up on the text.

"She asked if I was the mysterious conference contact that you'd been texting like a fiend."

He laughed. "'Like a fiend'? Maria said that?" Incredulous, he wondered what else his loose-lipped employee told her.

"So I'm a conference contact is all? That hurts," Hilary said, leaning forward. Her smile was bewitching.

Dane couldn't pass up the opportunity. He kissed her lightly, lingering to inhale the sweetness of her perfume. She drew a shaky breath and pulled away, her cheeks flushed.

"So, Jorie knows you're here?" he asked when he settled back in his chair.

"I didn't tell her directly, but I think she knew." Hilary took a strand of her hair and twisted it around her finger. "She wouldn't mind now."

Hilary filled him in on her conversations with Jorie, including their confrontation at the bank, and also the progress with the inn. He wasn't surprised to learn that most of Jorie's reservations and need for control had to do with her suppressed grief from losing her brother.

"I don't want to step away completely from the inn, but I don't want it to be everything to me. There are too many other things I want to do," she said.

Dane took her hand, caressing each of her fingers. Outside, the water cascading from the eaves had slowed to a steady drip. The sweet tang of lavender hung in the air. Hilary was studying him when he looked up.

"Do I fit into those plans of yours anywhere?" he asked.

From her expression, Dane knew the answer. But he wanted to hear the conviction in her voice.

She clasped his hands in hers and grinned.

"You fit into all of them."

Chapter Twenty-Three
EPILOGUE

Hilary stood over the farmhouse sink, letting the faucet fill up the empty casserole pan to soak, while staring through the window. Outside, the early morning sun hit the dew-topped grass in golden radiance. She never tired of moments like this. A day full of promise beckoned, even though nothing special was planned. But Dane was upstairs in the Cortland room. That brightened her day immeasurably.

He'd come yesterday afternoon and would stay until after lunch. His visit was a short one this weekend; he needed to get back to the farm. They'd taken to alternating weekends—Hilary in Clove, Dane in Redville —to visit each other during the last year. It was less than five hours in good weather and a pretty drive on Route 26 through national forests, especially this time of year.

Jorie popped into the kitchen, dressed in running clothes, coffee mug in hand.

"Morning," she said with a quick smile.

Hilary shut off the water. "You look ready for the day. What are you up to?" She followed Jorie into the walk-in pantry where her sister-in-law began rummaging through one of the wicker baskets holding serving ware they rarely used. But the clatter of metal was too much. Hilary backed out of the small space and took refuge at the far end of the kitchen, massaging her temple.

"I have everything on the buffet, but I don't hear anyone stirring," Hilary called, though she doubted Jorie heard above the racket. "Are you sure you told them we serve breakfast at eight?" she asked, raising her voice.

"They know," she said over her shoulder. "I heard the people in Honeycrisp turn on the shower."

"I hate trying to keep stuff warm." Hilary winced again as more metal clanged together in the basket. "Maybe I'll put it back in the oven."

Jorie stopped digging. "Not necessary. By the way, I didn't see the fruit salad out there."

Hilary made a face. "That's because it wasn't on the menu. But I can get right on it."

"Fruit is on the bottom shelf of the fridge," said Jorie as she went back to digging. When Hilary didn't move right away, Jorie looked back at her. "You'd better hurry. They'll be down soon."

As she set the basket of strawberries, blueberries, and

peaches on the counter, Hilary grumbled under her breath. She wasn't supposed to be prepping everything by herself. Jorie usually took care of the fruit salad and other sides while Hilary made the casserole or whatever other main dish they offered for the breakfast buffet. It wasn't like Jorie to ignore her responsibilities for the morning routine.

Jorie shut the pantry door, stopping on her way into the dining room to look over Hilary's shoulder. "Looks good. Bring that out when you're finished, okay?"

Hilary almost said something before Jorie buzzed out of the room. Of course she'd bring it out after she was finished mixing the fruit. What else would she do with it? Maybe Jorie was dumping her responsibilities on Hilary since she'd spent most of yesterday with Dane. That never was an issue before today though.

Hilary rinsed the fruit in the colander before transferring it to a glass bowl. She carried it through the swinging doors into the dining room and made room on the already full buffet as the Granny Smith guests wandered into the room. Behind them, Jorie stood wringing her hands.

"Good morning," Hilary said to the couple from Miami. They had reserved their room for the week while visiting family in the area. "Whenever you're ready to eat is fine. Coffee and juice are on the serving cart to your right. Everything else is on the buffet."

Jorie hooked her finger at her. *Come here*, she mouthed.

She acted so strange and frankly, it was a little annoying. Hilary excused herself while their guests began to fill their plates.

"We have people here," Hilary whispered when they were in the front room and out of earshot.

"I'll take care of them," Jorie said. "I have breakfast for you on the porch."

Jorie crossed the room to the door with the fleur-de-lis stained glass window. It led to the tiny but charming side porch overlooking a crescent-shaped perennial garden of cosmos, lilies, and a trellis overflowing with purple clematis.

"Breakfast for me? But I've already eaten. We never eat while the guests are downstairs." She lifted her chin toward the dining room. Hilary looked Jorie up and down. "Sorry, but you're acting weird."

Jorie groaned. "Man, you're hard to manage." She pushed open the door, sweeping her hand toward the porch for Hilary. "Just get out here."

Hilary was about to protest again, but the air was infused with the scent of lavender. She stepped down onto the porch and stopped.

"What is this?"

A white tablecloth with crocheted edges was draped over the little oak table. Sometimes Hilary liked to sit out here when the inn was empty, enjoying her tea and reading. But the tablecloth was new and so was the vase of fresh flowers—zinnias, artemisia, and lavender.

Hilary walked over to the table and rubbed the blossoms between her fingers. "I didn't know Dane brought lavender with him."

"Neither did I until now. I'm just following orders."

Confused, Hilary ran her hand over the tablecloth, taking in the details.

"He asked you to do this?"

Jorie cranked the windows open so the crisp fall air wafted onto the porch.

"Yes. Stay here," she said, giving her a quick peck on the cheek. "Don't worry. The guests will be fine."

After Jorie left her, Hilary turned back to the table. It was set with the antique flow blue china that once belonged to Jorie's grandmother. There were clear hobnail juice glasses, footed glass dishes with yogurt and fruit, and a silver-plated serving dish in the middle of everything. Hilary leaned over to lift the lid.

"I wouldn't do that."

The lid clattered back into place. Hilary whirled around.

Dane leaned against the doorframe, his hands stuck in the pockets of his jeans. His hair was damp, a few wet curls pasted against his neck. The dark green flannel shirt stretched across his broad shoulders, which reminded Hilary of the first time she'd set eyes on him at the airport. The color of his hair had reminded her a little of Will's. Now that she'd gotten to know him, there was hardly any comparison, physical or otherwise.

"You scared me."

"Sorry," he said with a grin.

She bent over the table to smell the flowers. "Where were you hiding these?"

"They've been in my car since yesterday morning. I'll have to drive home with the windows open."

He came forward and hugged her to him. She felt his breath on her neck then a nibbling kiss on her earlobe. "I thought we could start the day with a little love and lavender," Dane said, his voice low and intoxicating. "Unless you'd rather go serve your guests."

Hilary turned her face toward his and let her lips linger on his mouth.

"Love and lavender. I like that," she said, then drew back. She didn't have the heart to tell him she'd already grabbed a quick breakfast of yogurt and a cinnamon-raisin bagel, her go-to meal on mornings when they had guests. But he didn't know her routine. There was still so much to learn about each other.

They'd taken it slow over the last year, visiting every month, texting and calling, getting to know each other in the tempered way of long-distance romances. She told him more about her life growing up in California and her short marriage to Will. He shared the details of Felicia's betrayal and his dreams for Lavender Lane Farms. The more they talked, the easier it was for Hilary to picture her future.

Since the heartfelt talk with Jorie after the conference

last year, Hilary had less anxiety about helping with the inn, at least temporarily. After she returned from the trip to visit her family, Hilary breathed easier and enjoyed the process of getting the inn ready for guests. She and Jorie welcomed their first booking seven months ago, a husband and wife celebrating their wedding anniversary. Since then, the six bedrooms were mostly filled, especially on weekends when the fall colors drew travelers through Redville and the surrounding state forests. The busyness of prepping for opening transitioned to an equally full calendar of hosting guests, but her new duties soothed her. She still dreamed of returning to schoolwork, but for now she was content.

Dane pulled out the nearest chair. "For you."

Hilary smiled, trying to keep the laughter from bubbling up. His formality tickled her. Their weekends consisted mostly of carry-out pizza or Thai at home, depending on if they were in Clove or Redville, and meals bought on their Saturday road trips around the countryside. They relished their alone time since it was rare. Sit-down meals with their extended families were even more scarce.

"Thank you." She reached toward the silver serving dish again. "What do we have here?"

Dane's hand covered hers in an instant. "Patience. We have all morning." He pushed her yogurt closer. "Let's start with this."

She studied him. Dane was up to something again.

His understated sense of humor always surprised her. Sometimes she didn't catch on until she heard the familiar "Hil, it's a joke." She always played along, but she didn't want any more yogurt now. She'd eaten enough during her first breakfast. Reluctantly, she picked up her spoon.

Dane avoided looking at her by busying himself with pouring juice, floating the napkin to his lap, and fiddling with his silverware. As hard as he tried, Hilary still saw the hint of merriment in the wrinkles near his eyes.

"What do you have planned for today after I leave?" he asked. Dane sipped his coffee and looked out the window in a show of nonchalance. He wasn't fooling anyone.

Fine. She'd go with the flow. Let him think he could pull one over on her. She didn't know what the surprise was, but the suspense in the room was thick.

"All the rooms are booked for tonight too. So I have to run to town for groceries. Then maybe help Jorie with the rooms she hasn't finished."

"And tomorrow?"

She sighed. The serving dish drew her attention again. Was her surprise under there? He'd made such a show of not letting her take off the lid. Twice.

"More of the same. Meal prep, cleaning. I'll probably round up some apples for baking."

"I take it the inn is pretty full for the rest of the week?"

"It's October. We've been booked for weeks." She might as well be carrying on a conversation with the serving dish since she couldn't take her eyes from it. She'd bet her bank account the surprise lay under the lid. Plus, this small talk of his was obviously a stall tactic.

He leaned back in his chair, crossing his arms. "I bet you'll be ready for a break after the month is over."

"I'm ready for one now." Hilary huffed and thumbed toward the dining room. "Someone keeps pushing everything off on me." She really should check on the guests if only to clear away dishes.

"Like what?"

Her patience exhausted, Hilary needed to know what he hid in the serving dish and she needed to know right now.

She stood, leaning over the table. "Listen, I'm just going to look under this lid."

Before he could stop her, she whipped off the lid, clanging it against the juice pitcher. Dane steadied it before it toppled.

He laughed. "Whoa! If I'd known you were this hungry, we could have eaten first and talked later."

Hilary stared dumbly at the pancakes. "This is it?"

"I thought you loved pancakes?" Dane's eyes were wide, the corners of his mouth downturned.

Embarrassment lit her face on fire. Hilary rolled her shoulders. She really needed a mental reset.

"I'm sorry. I thought—"

"What?" he asked as he used his fork to set a pancake on her plate.

"Never mind."

Dane shrugged while he served himself.

"Maybe it's the short weekend. I wish you didn't have to leave so soon." She slathered her pancake with butter then passed the knife to him.

"I know. I'm sorry. This next week will be so busy." He pointed to the serving dish with his fork. "What did you think was under there?"

She lifted her shoulder. "Nothing...just breakfast."

"I see."

Dane poked at the fruit in his dish. He lifted a strawberry to his mouth while a little grin crinkled his eyes.

"Tell me again what you have going on?" Hilary vaguely remembered him talking about traveling to meet new vendors. It sounded ideal. If only she weren't tied down here she'd tag along. She so needed a vacation.

"There's a honey farmer near Hermiston whose products Maria has had on her radar for a while. She's talked me into stocking some at the store. They invited me to come up, check out their operation. They also have an inn on their property."

Hilary frowned. "I'm jealous."

Dane grinned his slow, one-sided smile that never failed to send a rush of desire through her.

"Then come with," he said.

"I wish." She scanned the table for syrup. "There's too much to do."

"You haven't had a vacation since the conference. If that could even be counted as one."

"Vacation? What's that?" Hilary laughed. She pushed her chair away from the table. "I'm going to get some syrup."

Dane pointed again with his fork. "It's on the cart behind you. I brought some of our new lavender vanilla syrup. I think you'll like it."

Sure enough. A dainty glass jug sat on the antique tea cart against the wall. She grasped it and set it on the table in front of her. The Lavender Lane logo sticker on the front made her smile. He'd even tied a thin purple bow around the handle. It was so—

Her breath caught.

Hilary leaned closer as if the object a foot away wasn't obvious enough. She squinted at it as her heart *thunk-thunked* in her chest.

Looped through the ribbon was a ring.

A gold one with a diamond.

When she glanced at him, his wide smile made his eyes almost disappear above his cheeks.

He shrugged, glancing down at his plate again as he sliced through a pancake. "Maybe you won't like it. Lavender vanilla isn't—"

"Dane?"

He stopped. "Yes?"

"Why are you talking about syrup?" Joy made her voice waver.

His hearty laugh shook his shoulders, and he slid out of his chair and kneeled beside her in an instant.

"Because you're so easy to tease." He took her hand, resting their intertwined fingers in her lap. "Because those dimples above your cheeks when you smile drive me crazy. Because I want to spend a lifetime making you laugh. Because I love you."

Tears blurred her vision. She'd been waiting for this moment. They'd talked about their future since their first month together. It wasn't a matter of *if* they'd get married but when. Dane liked his surprises, though, so she hadn't pressed him for a timeline.

Dane untied the ribbon from the jug handle, letting the ring fall into his hand. He slipped it onto her finger with a little trouble. His hand shook despite the carefree grin.

"I think you know what this means, right?"

"Yes," she said simply, wrapping her arms around his neck. She held her hand up behind his head, admiring the ring. Hilary drew him close. "It means we won't have to spend our weeks apart anymore."

He kissed her. The heady combination of the lavender arrangement on the table and the softness of his lips brushing against hers made her head swim. Outside, a breeze stirred the chimes on the porch.

Dane drew back. The light in his dark eyes danced. "It also means you'll finally get a vacation. A long one."

Hilary tightened her arms around him.

She sighed. "Finally."

ARE YOU READY TO READ LOVE, LIES AND Mistletoe? Come back to Blueberry Point Lodge for the Christmas season! Interior designer Layla Dean receives a misdirected text invitation to a holiday event from Brant Johnsson, the same man she shared an awkward mistletoe encounter with at a fundraiser a year ago. Now they're together again, decking the inn for the holidays, and Layla hopes to avoid a repeat of that kiss even if dreamy Brandt hopes for a very merry second chance.

Acknowledgments

I'm so thankful for the cast of special people in my life who make writing and publishing books possible. These would include a wonderfully supportive group of writers whom I also call dear friends in our IG group: Sarah, Rachael, Marika, Daria, Dave, DeAnn, Gigi, IreAnne, Kayla, Melissa, Laura, Wendy, and Emily. Also, my lovely copy editor Hollie Westring, who has been with me almost from the beginning; and T.L who helped fill in the early holes in this story. I'd also love to give a special shout-out to Shaela Odd at Blue Water Books for the phenomenal cover design. I'm so excited I get to work with her on this series. Finally, I'd like to thank my family for their unwavering love and support, which keeps the words flowing.

Sign up for my newsletter at www.demalone.com to get up-to-the-minute book news, special subscriber deals, and other bookish fun including an exclusive content.

Also by D.E. Malone

Hearts in Hendricks series

Love Like Water #1

Love Like Fire #2

Love Like Air #3

Love Like Forever #4

Blueberry Point Romance series

Love, Lies and Lavender #1

Love, Lies and Mistletoe #2

Love, Lies and Lullabies #3

Love, Lies and Lemon Pie #4

Blueberry Point Romance Collection (novellas)

Love Between the Lines (free novella)

A Forever Kiss in Silver Leaf Falls

Middle Grade (writing as Dawn Malone)

Bingo Summer

The Upside of Down

About the Author

D.E. Malone writes contemporary romance and is the author of the Hearts in Hendricks series. She also writes for middle grade audiences as Dawn Malone. Her work has appeared in the Chicken Soup for the Soul series, *Highlights for Children*, and numerous magazines and newspapers. When not writing, she loves spending time outdoors in the gardens, hiking, and exploring places off-the-beaten path. She lives in central Illinois surrounded by corn and soybean fields. She can be found on Facebook, Instagram, and Goodreads as dmalonebooks. Visit her website at https://www.demalone.com.

Made in the USA
Middletown, DE
10 March 2023

26546554R00146